WHEN THE WAVE COLLAPSES

NORAH WOODSEY

Copyright 2016 by Norah Woodsey, norahwoodsey.com

ISBN 978-0-9973339-4-7
eBook ISBN 978-0-9973339-3-0

Cover by Chris Bentham

Author photograph by Lauren Naylors
lnaylor.com

For Beans and Tobes. Thank you for joining me in this reality.

DISCLAIMER

Our universe does not appear in this story.

NOVEMBER 11, 2003

9:04 PM

JULIE COYNE PRESSED HER PALMS FLAT ON THE METAL lab table and read the data again. In a separate channel of her brain, she noted her assistants shuffling backwards on the linoleum floor as their conversations fell to whispers, then died. The computer screen reflected their nervous tics or downcast eyes, but she didn't acknowledge them. She didn't notice the plume of vapor released onto the table by the heat and sweat of her palms, either. She kept her focus on the data.

She lifted her hands and moved them over the keyboard. Her fingertips traced the letters, soft shapes rising gently against the ridges of her skin. Her breathing remained steady as the data populated in white characters against a black background. There was nothing new to examine. There was no one to blame and no one to turn to if she made the wrong choice. Julie took a moment to admire the lines of code, each symbol evidence of other worlds brought into this one by her work.

Here was her accomplishment. She did this, whatever it was.

Julie stole a glance toward the back of the lab. Emitting heat and receiving signals that could not be traced, insensible to the chaos it caused, Gordon the machine continued humming. Julie typed the command. Clenching her jaw, she hit ENTER.

DECEMBER 3, 2020

11:46 AM

THEY WERE TOGETHER AGAIN. LISE EXTENDED HER legs on the scratchy hall runner, happy to observe. Sophie's glossy brown curls shined in the sunlight, the spirals dancing on her tiny shoulders as she retrieved blocks from a pile of toys. Elliot made faces for his own amusement in their stepmother's tall mirror. Lise gave in to temptation, quickly embracing her sister in a loving squeeze. The toddler tolerated the interruption momentarily. The three of them were playing in the downstairs hall as they used to do on rainy days. The walls of their block castle had tiny flags that fluttered in a breeze she could not feel. It drew Lise's confused attention, but then Elliot knocked over one of Sophie's creations.

"Lise, I want to go upstairs!" he demanded.

Lise smiled, not wanting to scold him, and gave him a kiss on the head before he darted up the steps. She tried to follow, lifting tiny Sophie. But instead of rising easily into her arms as she always had, the girl slid down. Elliot continued to climb the stairs, higher and higher. Lise couldn't follow.

It seemed like she could find a solution, if only he would wait. Lise tried to call to him, but he couldn't hear her. With a bit of adjusting, it felt like she had a firmer grip on her sister. Lise looked up and saw that the stairs were either moving higher or the floor beneath her feet was sinking. She looked down and saw blankets pooled at her feet. The toy blocks were gone. It didn't matter why there were blankets instead of blocks. Lise felt Sophie's little hands slide down her arms and watched the toddler slowly disappearing into the darkness of the sinking floor. Lise looked up to see Elliot fading into the shadows of the lengthening stairwell.

Lise heard Sophie's tiny voice begging her to stay, Elliot shouting something. She struggled to go back to sleep to finish what she'd started. To pull her, to climb back up to him . . . but first she needed something. Something important. It was up above. Or did she have it already? Maybe a ladder would help, but it was rickety. She could almost feel the wooden rungs in her hands.

The dream, once all consuming, dissolved in her building consciousness, the voices of her beloved siblings fading from her ears.

Lise tried to burrow into her blankets, but there was no sleep for her there. She wiped the tears from her eyes and stared out the window. By the light on the leafless plum tree, she guessed it was almost noon. Eventually she swung her feet over the side of her bed into her slippers. The freshly waxed floor was bitterly cold. The past four winters hadn't been nearly so brutal. That the cold wasn't accompanied by snow always came as a surprise. It used to snow up here. There was an abandoned ski lodge on the other side of the hills, deep in Arapahoe National Forest. Now it was just cold. Cold and unbearably dry.

She put on the robe that hung on the back of her door. Moving down the single hallway, she entered the open room that served as the living, dining, and kitchen area. She walked to the kitchen wedged into the corner and turned the knob on the stovetop. The burner chirped its familiar click, click, click greeting before bursting into flames. She grabbed the kettle she had filled the night before and set it over the flames. From one of her three cupboards, she pulled out her only mug. Beside it were a plate, a bowl, and the glass that held her silverware. At another cupboard, Lise's eyes passed over cans of food, bags of grain, and bottles of vitamins and settled on her small tins of tea. It was difficult and expensive to have tea delivered from overseas, but having something special made her happy. Today called for something new.

The sound of tires on gravel nearly caused her to drop the tin can. She froze, listening. The sounds were not immediately outside. Lise tightened her robe and moved to the front window, peering through a gap in the plywood slats. At the front door of the main house, a few hundred feet from Lise's shabby little porch, a man in a brown uniform dropped a package at the doorstep, then looked around. He crossed the porch to peek into the window. Lise wondered what he thought about delivering goods to an abandoned house. No one ever suspected the forlorn in-law unit out back of being the sole occupant's principle dwelling. A noise in the forest beyond the house startled him. He left quickly, as expected.

The box looked about the size that should accommodate her book orders. The bookcases lining her walls were full, save two shelves toward the bottom. Regular internet access would have made such a collection unnecessary, but that was a luxury Lise could not safely enjoy. No phones, no television, no internet. Not after what happened last time.

Yet the box waiting within sight of her front door was proof that she wasn't being as cautious as she should be. In the early days, her shipments were delivered to a vacant house down the hillside, and she would spirit them away in the night, safe from curious delivery men. Uneventful years had made her careless. The kettle whistled pleasantly and Lise attended to it before it started to scream.

While her drink turned from wisps of copper floating in hot water to dark brown tea, Lise made a plate of preserves and whole-grain crackers. She planned out the rest of her day: research, chores, and when darkness set in, the box.

In some ways, she took comfort in the isolation. She had loved her mother, loved her siblings, but she lost them. There was no one she missed but them. As a child, she'd wanted the satisfaction school friendships brought to others, but whenever she tried to fit in, join a new lunch table, attend a birthday party, hang out under a certain tree after class, she felt out of place and even more alone. With such steady rejection, solitude became a relief. After class, she would go home to her mother, to her siblings, and find everything she needed from the world in their arms.

With a spoon covered in honey, she set her teacup on a saucer at the small handcrafted table. She pulled her book toward her. Slips of paper and dog-ears were her way of prioritizing information now that she needed to conserve power and paper; the delivery man couldn't be summoned often or he would get comfortable browsing the grounds. There was another way to get supplies, but the thought sickened her. Whatever it took, she wouldn't resort to that. Even if it meant dog-earing pages in her book.

Hours passed as the words on the pages blocked out her surroundings. She didn't think about the moldy smell she could never quite get rid of. She didn't notice the whispering breeze coming in through the gaps in the windows and door. Her free hand fidgeted with her biggest keloidal scar, on her left shoulder, as she read.

In time, she grabbed a blanket and relocated to the back porch for the afternoon light. College textbooks and assigned readings had failed her long ago; in recent months, she'd been sifting through pages of conspiracy babble. She read an entire series of books only to discover they were useless. This one, a collection of magazine essays, was peppered with information that seemed useful. Her highlighter was uncapped in anticipation as she turned to the next chapter:

PARALLEL UNIVERSES: TRANSPORTING OBJECTS THROUGH TELEKINESIS

Lise highlighted the heading. Years ago, she'd read an article in a science magazine discussing how energy from other universes could be detected with sensitive equipment. The study had started as an attempt to entangle two particles, but the experimenters soon realized that each particle already had its own partner, nearby or elsewhere. In passing, the author mentioned that this could explain some supernatural phenomena—a note for which he was probably ridiculed by his colleagues. Lise didn't simply *accept* the idea of gaps in human understanding; that was where she lived and breathed.

The chapter didn't contain what she was looking for, though. She threw the book to the side, capped her highlighter furiously and tossed it to the floor. She gathered her robe around her and adjusted the blanket. At times like this she wished she had a smoking habit. Solitude was a comfort, but boredom was oppressive. Smoking made sitting alone seem purposeful.

After a moment, she found a way to rest her head that was almost comfortable. She forgot about her dream, her box of books, her research, her loneliness, and she sank into the silence of the forest. During winter, the animals moved deeper into the woods to hibernate. Turned away by the frigid temperatures and dry air, hikers were rare. In later months, Lise would hide indoors despite the oppressive heat. A startled animal could reveal her location, and hikers often tried to explore the "abandoned" property. She had put up intimidating No Trespassing signs with rusty barbed wire, along with Vicious Dog warnings and Right to Bear Arms propaganda, but it didn't always work. Some people seemed encouraged by them, particularly teenagers. They were horror-movie victims for a reason.

She let her head fall back against her chair, closed her eyes, and felt the soft forest breeze brush her face as she sank slowly to sleep.

3

———————

SEPTEMBER 16, 2012

7:13 PM

Daniel leaned against a support post in his uncle's pawn shop, waiting for the next set of instructions. His fingers discovered a hole in his front pocket where his keys had cut the material. He scowled. This had been his nice pair of jeans, but this new hole matched the two at the backs of his cuffs where his heels had rubbed away the fabric. He'd been doing a lot of walking lately.

To get to class, he had to experience downtown in all its glory. The mornings found him speeding past prostitutes and drug dealers on his way to the bus stop. After a mile on the 59X route, he shuffled past manicured landscapes to the polished stone steps of the private university. After class, he took the bus back to his neighborhood, dodging through the city's late-afternoon cast of undesirables. Once home, he went to work replacing stock in his uncle's pawn shop. There were a lot of opportunities for holes to form at the cuffs of his jeans.

He could ignore those, but he relied on his front pockets. Pickpockets tended to go for back pockets. Of course, muggers just took whatever you had, front pockets or no.

This hole explained how he lost some of his change for the laundromat the night before. He'd had to walk all the way home with his dirty laundry to get more. He'd have to patch it up when he had time.

Hazy memories of shopping for school clothes surfaced. His mom had always found shopping annoying, so Dad took the kids at the start of each term. By the time Daniel was old enough to have opinions about his clothes, his sisters were shopping on their own. Shopping with his dad then became a guy-bonding thing; they'd hit the sports bar and get burgers, then wrap up their trip with a stop in the comic book shop in the downtown promenade. His dad always bought something funny for Mom. Even when Daniel thought it was dorky, his mom loved it. He smiled at the memory and then pushed it aside. That was his past now.

If he really needed something, he could ask his uncle, but he would never ask for new clothes. Most teenagers from his background who survived the pandemic and the violence that followed were homeless or in shelters. He was one of the lucky ones. Guilt weighed down the want of new clothes. Even with all his work around the shop, Daniel knew he was a burden. He'd been with Uncle Joe for three years since his parents and sisters died. No one else had offered to help. Daniel would always remember that.

His uncle muttered profanities to himself as he sat on the floor beside a large box, surrounded by cheap imitations of nice objects. He wiped his face with a handkerchief.

"Danny, do me a favor. This fucking thing is dirty. Get me the cleaner and a paper towel, will you?"

Daniel nodded and quickly passed from the shelves to the metal security gate, opened the door, and went to the back of the shop. He returned with a handful of rags and an old bottle of window cleaner that now contained mystery soap. His uncle grunted a thank you and cleaned the bookend in his hand.

Uncle Joe was in his fifties, formerly muscular but now made up of large, rounded shapes. His arms were decorated with military tattoos that had stretched and faded to a pale emerald. His head was probably the least hairy area on his body. He wore a chain around his neck with a pendant of St. Anthony of Padua and a wedding band; both were obscured by a patch of chest hair. He'd been married once, long before Daniel could remember. Daniel's only image of Aunt Sylvia was from the family photos in his parents' hallway. His favorite was from a forgotten cousin's garden wedding. Daniel's parents, younger and clearly drunk, stood next to Uncle Joe and Aunt Sylvia. Sylvia's cloud of tight blond curls dated the photo. Joe's tattoos were probably fresh under his crisp dress shirt. His face was thin, tan, and perfectly happy as he held his laughing wife in a half-hug.

Daniel recalled his mother crying as she told him about Sylvia's death. Years had passed since then, but the pain hadn't lost its edge. His mom described Sylvia's beauty, wit, and kindness, and how she died in Joe's arms. The Memorial Day terrorist attack that destroyed three tourist destinations on the eastern seaboard was now a brief footnote in news stories about politics and the economy: "Only fifteen people were killed in these attacks; hundreds die every day in British Honduras"—or some other unstable region. It made Daniel angry. One of those faceless fifteen, reduced from souls with lives and hopes and dreams to a sum, had been his aunt. The attacks killed Sylvia and ruined his uncle's life. Uncle Joe never spoke about her, and he never removed the necklace.

Joe finished wiping down the bookends and the shelf, tossing the rag into the box. He groped for something substantial enough to hold his weight as he rose from the floor. Daniel would have offered to help him up but he knew Joe wouldn't have it. The winner was a large, empty gumball dispenser. It tottered under the strain but stayed upright as Joe stood.

"Uncle Joe, how about you just point to where you want things to go and I'll clean them up and put them away."

Joe nodded, wiping his forehead with his ever-present handkerchief. Daniel took his uncle's place at the large box and pushed it along as they moved to the next shelf. The box caught on imperfections in the dark old wood floorboards, which wore the scars from thousands of shoes. Oblong indents from high heels pierced some soft spots; drag marks from heavy objects gouged curved lines into other places. In the decades since they were installed, countless desperate souls had walked across their ridges to the security fence and the bulletproof glass wall that protected the cashier.

Impoverished people used to come in a slow but steady trickle, familiar with the process of selling their remaining valuables to pay down title loans or get their power turned back on. Since the pandemic, though, all kinds of people came in. The city's former middle class came in clutching electronics and jewelry seeking funds to buy food. Scary people with addictions nourishing their poverty had grown common, shifting in agitation as they sold anything they could find or steal. Even with the security glass and screen, Daniel usually gave those people more than their items were worth in hopes they'd quickly go away.

He finished a shelf and began pushing the box to the next section. Uncle Joe frowned. "Be careful with that box, there's some china plates at the bottom there. I didn't pack it too good."

"They aren't even real."

"Danny, they're real enough to make us money,

so just shut up, will you?" There was no menace in his uncle's tone, only annoyance and fatigue.

The two progressed up and down the aisles, transferring the price tags they had written up earlier to each item's space on the shelf. One light-up toy had a name scrawled faintly in crayon on the bottom. A necklace had a single strand of hair caught in the clasp. Fingerprints muted the sheen of a heavy brass desk clock. Daniel tried not to think of who used to own the things he carried. Some had been loved possessions. He thought of all the stuff he left behind when he moved here. Was a dog chewing on one of his dad's favorite shoes? Was someone wearing Mom's wedding dress?

Daniel paused and surveyed his surroundings. It was growing dark. Lamplight from the street corner cast a blue glow on the gun case. There were two hunting rifles, six handguns, and a shotgun in the illuminated, red-velvet-backed glass case. Outside, a bottle shattering on the pavement briefly interrupted an argument between two drunks. Daniel set a pendulum with seven steel balls on the shelf in front of his face, the metal tinkling as they bounced into one another in an erratic pattern. The ball in the center remained still. Daniel reached into the box for another object. He looked back at the gun case.

"Uh, did a handgun fall off a peg?"

Uncle Joe grimaced and glanced over at the gun case. "No."

Daniel waited for his uncle to elaborate, but he remained focused on organizing the books in front of him.

"I thought I saw six guns in there. There are only five now."

"You probably did. That's the ghost."

Daniel's smile faded. "The ghost?"

"Yeah. I told you this place was haunted."

"No, you told me to tell my friends this place was haunted so they'd stay away. You never told ME this place was haunted."

"I see. Sorry. The shop is haunted."

"In what way?"

"In what way? What a stupid question. In the 'there's a ghost that steals stuff' sort of way, kid. Jesus, what are they teaching you at that school."

"But . . . where does the stuff go?"

"They don't take anything with GPS."

Daniel stopped speaking. The growing darkness, the pleasant promise of the end of the workday was now menacing. A slight settling sound in the far corner made him wary. He looked to the stairs leading to the apartment above, eager to run to the safety of a familiar space. Uncle Joe saw his look and smiled.

"Relax. I've never seen anything spooky. Stuff just goes missing. It's the gun cabinet, mostly, but sometimes it's other stuff too. Lost my first aid kit from under the register once."

"But it's not, like, just misplaced or something?"

Uncle Joe laughed. "You can't misplace a samurai sword and a shotgun. This has been going on a long, long time. Even the old baker I bought the place from went through this. His flour and eggs and rolling pins and whatever disappeared. Drove him nuts, he never knew how much to keep in stock. It's why I got the place so cheap. Your school wanted to buy up all the buildings on this block years back, you know. No clue why, in this neighborhood. They backed out last minute. I guess they were too superstitious."

"Have you had it investigated, or, I mean, reported it?"

"Kid, I don't run the sort of place where I can be calling the cops, you know what I'm saying? Besides, no one gives two shits about ghosts right now. The world is going to hell in a handbasket. Nobody cares."

Daniel nodded and returned to his work. He put labels in their places and adjusted items on shelves. He looked over at the gun cabinet warily, then at his uncle, who had gone back to work. The tingling sensation on his neck hadn't faded yet. Maybe it never would.

4

NOVEMBER 10, 2003

2:55 PM

JULIE LISTENED TO MARSHALL'S ATTEMPT TO reproach her with the interest she would pay to someone driving a car with a manual transmission. The high-pitched complaining accelerated until he changed gears to somber disappointment. Occasionally he'd regain her interest by mistiming a shift and stammering at her incoherently for a brief moment before he found his rhythm again. She tried to look bland and accepting, with appropriate fluctuations into concerned apology. The wall clock behind him begged for attention, but she kept her eyes away from it. This was a familiar dance for both of them.

They had been classmates in undergrad. Marshall Corrigan's face sometimes brought her back to when they were teenagers. They had never been equals. In college, she lived in a roach-infested studio at a motel converted to apartments; he lived in a physics and mathematics fraternity house. Julie didn't apply herself as much as she could have, maintaining friendships and even a love life, while Marshall seemed to do nothing but study. After their late-night lab groups, they'd discuss their projects and walk together through the dark, quiet campus until they reached the statue of the university's founder at the base of a grassy hill. They had never bothered to read the plaque. From there the path branched off in three directions. They would awkwardly nod or wave goodnight. Marshall went one way, Julie went another, and the third path was always dark, empty, and foreboding.

On the day of their graduation, Julie waited for Marshall's name to be called. The audience had been instructed not to applaud until all the names had been read, but everyone ignored the rules. Before the speaker finished reading Marshall's name and honors, she'd stood, whistling and clapping for him as he crossed the stage and collected his diploma. He scanned the crowd and paused mid-stride to smile at her. It was a unfamiliar smile, a meaning behind it she couldn't articulate. Sometimes the warm shock it gave her resurfaced. After the ceremony, she looked for him, but he was lost in the crowd.

They went to different graduate schools but stayed in touch over IRC and group emails. Julie opted for a less strenuous molecular physics PhD program with independent work and a study-abroad component. Diligent as ever, Marshall chose a prestigious research university's particle physics program and the most unforgiving faculty member as his advisor.

Now Marshall was the youngest scientist ever given leadership over the physical sciences wing at Bresling University, and Julie ran a research lab in his department. Some people thought she might resent him for it, that hers was another tale of sexism and woe, but she assured them that didn't apply here. She hadn't put in the work, and she wasn't interested in politicking for authority. There were challenges he had faced, sacrifices he'd made, to get where he was today. When he was in a position to recruit researchers, he called her and gave her a job offer her résumé didn't justify. As long as he left her to do her work, she felt happy for him.

Julie woke from her thoughts and checked the clock meaningfully. Marshall sighed and paused to prepare his usual post-reprimand summary.

"You need results. You know John is getting anxious. This equipment isn't cheap, and you're using a lot of our computer power and time in Kyle's lab. He has his own work to do and year-end reviews are coming up. Okay?"

"Sure thing, boss."

Julie walked down the hallway, shaking her head at the flickering fluorescent light, the battered yellow paint, and the dingy gray linoleum. In the movies, a research university of this caliber would be pristine white with large glass enclosures, perfect lighting, and automatic sliding doors. Everyone would be beautiful and serious in starched lab coats. Most people didn't realize this world-renowned physics research facility used grocery-store tin foil on Faraday cages and cheap rubber wedges to keep the ill-fitting doors closed during experiments. Two rooms from the end of the hall, she could see the sign posted on her lab. Someone had scotch-taped a drawing of a sealed box with the words "Speak to me, cat!" across the side.

No one greeted her as she entered the lab. The large room was divided into two sections. Directly in front of her, shelving units reached the ceiling. Her own small desk was squeezed in at the end of the aisle next to the only window in the room. A gap in the shelving behind her chair made the space just barely functional. To the right of the door was a pathway to a long, built-in desk that held the computer stations for the graduate students: Allison Evans, a structural engineer; and Xiulan Zhang, a particle physicist. Opposite them sat Spencer Klepin, a software engineer and post-doc physicist who had set up his very neat and very small desk across the room.

Alone, on the farthest wall, was the machine. As a prototype it had been given the name Gordon. That was when it rested on a table, but subsequent modifications had made it too large and heavy. The table now loomed ominously against the wall, its structural supports like the retracted legs of a mechanical insect. Gordon hovered over a cooling pad on the floor. Back when Gordon was almost cute, before its inaugural power-up seven months earlier, a yellow half-octagon had been taped to the linoleum. Now the yellow line signaled real danger, the blackened edges of the warped tile around the cooling pad a cautionary tale.

Spencer was hunched in his typical stance, typing and bouncing his leg. Allison was standing near her workstation holding an apple and snapping her gum as she waited for the scale to calibrate. Xiulan was inside the boundary, examining the test area and using a canister of compressed air to dust off the grid etched into the platform. It wasn't necessary, but Julie said nothing. While this was an experiment, no one expected to move the apple. Perhaps a part of the apple, a collection of molecules from the apple; not the entire fruit. But her team was like her, not satisfied with incremental advances.

She moved to her corner, the worst desk in the room, and her elbow narrowly missed the shelf. With movements refined by habitual action, she quickly opened her flimsy cubby and switched out her plain brown glasses for her bright blue pair. It made her feel a bit like Mr. Rogers to have glasses for each occasion.

"Dr. Coyne, we're ready to run Gordon."

The others were already shutting off machines, most of the lights, and the sleeping computers. They blew a fuse last time they powered Gordon up, so this time they were shutting off all nonessentials. Julie shut off her monitor and tower.

Only Spencer's computer was needed for the first stage. Once Gordon's capacitors were fully charged, they could start turning things back on.

Julie left her desk and walked over to examine the machine as the lab assistants bustled around her. All the power supplies, cooling lines, and data cables seemed to be connected. Circuit boards were bright and clean, safely concealed behind plexiglass. The gleaming new power supply on the back of Gordon's housing shone in self-satisfaction. The top of the unit looked like an old overhead projector on steroids. Julie smiled at the arts-and-craftsy nature of the machine. Their budget was healthy for a research study, but insufficient for a project of this scale. A large inheritance from Julie's grandfather had covered much of the foundational expenses, including most of the rare metals. That meant anything beyond sensitive equipment required ingenuity.

Julie went back to her station and grabbed her audio recorder. She touched her little porcelain good-luck cat Xiulan had ironically gifted to everyone. The others did the same. She hit Record.

"Dr. Julie Coyne. Running sequence alpha. Time is 3:27 p.m., date is November 10th, 2003. This is our fourth attempt. First following modifications to the power supply and upgraded shielding on data cables. Nearby lab conducting dysprosium thermalization may have caused some interference in the three previous trials. All right, Allison, place the test subject. Spence, get ready to run program."

Allison placed the apple on the scale, recording the measurement before moving the fruit to the optimistically named "launch pad." Spencer looked over to Gordon, muttered something under his breath, and went back to his screen. Xiulan flipped off the last few power strips in the darkened room, then rolled the giant metal protective plates onto black Xs taped to the floor. Julie, Allison, and Xiulan took positions behind the solid screens, shifting their gazes between Spencer's monitor and the apple's reflection in a mirror mounted on the ceiling. Dangling from the machine was a plastic name tag with the words "Gordon's Free, Man" stamped in black letters on a white background.

"Running program," Spencer announced. The tag made its customary rattle. Without looking up, he spoke again over the powerful hum. "Searching for a connection."

The three women waited, watching the apple anxiously although they knew nothing was supposed to happen yet. They had spent three weeks updating Gordon's labyrinthine innards. Everyone in the room mentally reviewed their work, checking for missing screws or poor soldering. Occasionally, Julie would look at the empty receiving platform. Her anticipation was tempered by their previous failures, by all the unknowns in this study, and yet hope remained strong. She often wondered if pregnant women felt like this at the first serious pain of labor.

"Connection established. Waiting for synchronization."

Spencer's normally docile voice was tense. In the last trial runs, Gordon hadn't established a connection. Xiulan and Allison watched the apple eagerly. Julie closed her eyes.

"Loading."

Julie stopped breathing. She opened her eyes.

The apple was intact and exactly where they had left it. All waited silently for several moments. Julie let out a breath.

"Well, shit," Spencer muttered.

DECEMBER 3, 2020

5:50 PM

LISE WOKE OUTSIDE ON THE PORCH, HER CHIN STIFF with dried saliva. Embarrassed at herself, she retreated into the cold house. She made a fresh cup of tea and debated starting a fire. It wasn't dark enough yet to retrieve the box, so it definitely wasn't dark enough to start a fire. She had already been careless by sleeping outside. It was best to wait.

She threw logs into the old stone fireplace, arranged some kindling then struck a match. Tendrils of golden red curls retreated into the recesses of the wood. She was being reckless again; she wondered if her period was coming early. With a glance she noted that her woodpile was running low. Another trip deeper into the forest was on the horizon.

Once the fire was self-sustaining, she retreated a few feet, eager for the heat. Light still streamed in from the boarded-up front windows, the darkness slowly deepening. She'd have to light a couple lanterns soon. Geese flew high overhead, honking to one another as they raced over the treetops, little families traveling together to safety and plenty, far away from these woods. Lise relaxed as the warmth spread over her skin.

A knock at the door crashed into her.

Lise shuffled toward the back of the house, unable to summon the strength to stand. *It's not possible. I've been so careful.* Backing around the corner into the coat closet, she closed her eyes and strained to listen. Two people were muttering to one another. She thought she heard the words "definitely home" and "fire." They knocked again, louder this time.

Lise was shaking with adrenaline. She tried to focus on her surroundings. The smell of the musty coats. The button she needed to sew onto the black one. *Calm down*, she told herself. *Be calm.* A deep, slow inhale through her mouth. A slow, steady exhale through her nose. Pause for thirty seconds, then repeat.

The unwanted visitors knocked on the window, the glass threatening to shatter in its frame. Lise squeaked, her exhale went ragged. She shut her eyes tighter, attempting to refocus: the air tumbling through the recesses in her mouth and throat, then rushing to escape over the membranes of her nose. Her lungs swelling again with fresh air, her ribcage expanding as the blood in her body exchanged gases. At the precipice of oxygen depletion, she gave way to relief as she released the waste gases back to the world. Though she could hear more speaking, she wouldn't listen. She was of the world: she was in control. The last glimmers of light from the kitchen window were faintly visible through her closed eyes. The crackle of logs in the fire. The feel of the wooden board under her right hand. The cold metal in her left.

No, please. That can't be right, she begged herself, feeling the angry tears coalesce. *It can't be. No.*

Lise slowly opened her eyes and lifted the heavy object in her left hand. A handgun. Without checking, she knew it was loaded. Using all of her strength, she suppressed the desire to throw it. The sounds of retreating footsteps helped her calm down. Keeping the gun far from her body, she peeked around the corner. A little girl hiking with her mother. Wearily, she clicked the safety on and shut the weapon behind the closet door. Her relief was brief and weak. The gun couldn't stay there. She retrieved it and took it into an empty room. From a dark corner, she dragged a ladder over and climbed up. She pushed a panel in the ceiling up and aside. Concealed in the dark attic was a pile of knives, swords, guns of various sizes and dimensions. She added the handgun to the collection and closed the panel again.

Lise was still shaking when she returned to the front room. She paced for a moment, repeatedly checking the windows and doors. There was nothing more she could do. She folded herself down on the faded carpet in front of the fireplace. Another failure.

An unbidden memory arose in her mind. When she was a small girl, she went to a pool party with her pregnant mother. Her mother was beautiful, incredibly intelligent, funny yet quiet. She made friends easily. Eager to show off, Lise stood around awkwardly in her new bathing suit and waited for a break in the adults' conversation. Once she had just enough of the group's attention, she dove into the pool.

She hadn't checked the depth. Her pride at executing an elegant, splash-free dive died when her head struck the concrete floor. The meaning of up and down disappeared. Her limbs seemed to float on their own in the water. Consciousness faded. All around her was an endless pale blue, cold and surreal, enveloping her and growing dim.

Lise remembered her mother's arms around her in a fierce hug that brought her to the surface. She coughed and clung tightly as they climbed to the steps and sat down together. Blood from the gash in her forehead trickled steadily down and obscured her vision. She rested her head against her mother's swollen belly and watched the clouds of red bursting to life in the pure pool water.

Like a movie reel, the memory abruptly ended. Lise turned to the photo of her mother on the mantel. Her ghost appeared as perfection in Lise's memory. The beautiful baker who cooked whatever crazy recipes her children stumbled upon. She remembered the low, soft tones in which she sang to Lise's brother and sister. Lise had tried to sing those songs to them after she was gone. Crying through her own anger and loneliness and pain, she'd tried to soothe their broken hearts, but always felt like a failure.

This power, this disease, started a month after her mother's death. The three children were curled up in Lise's bed. Their father, with only the pretense of discretion, was out with the woman who would soon be their stepmother. Sophie had fallen asleep on her lap, the first time she had slept soundly in days. Elliot was crying, unable to find his Thomas the Tank Engine book. It had been a favorite, a popup book he had outgrown, but it had been a gift from Mommy. With a whimper, he asked Lise to find it for him. She couldn't risk waking Sophie. She shut her eyes and wished she had found it earlier; that it was in the bookcase, or under the bed, or on the bedside table.

It didn't appear in any of those places. When she opened her eyes, it was in her hands. Then, as many times afterward, it was slightly different. Their book she found weeks later, buried in a toy box. This copy had the outline of a library barcode sticker. The cover was a textured hardback with delicate pages, not their slick, childproof version.

Those differences hadn't mattered to Elliot, so they hadn't mattered to Lise. She read to him until he fell asleep. A thought crossed her mind as she held the two sleeping children and smiled for the first time since her mother's death. It was just the three of them, but now, somehow, she had a super-power. Their lives were going to be better. They could move away, leave their father to his "impor-tant meetings" that lasted all night, and start over in new schools where no one knew them.

That was before their father found out. Sophie had let it slip, asking Lise for a special type of ce-real one morning. Lise had felt so stupid, letting Sophie see her work. The change in her father's de-meanor had been frightening. He examined the cupboards, went through her backpack and her bedroom. That was when she learned this thing had come from her mother. It was how she had killed herself.

Lise didn't know what kinds of experiments her mom had been put through. It had seemed to her at the time, a terrified, motherless girl sitting in a thin hospital gown in a frigid room, that anony-mous lab workers were re-running tests, not just trying things out. When she felt especially angry at her mom, she thought of her first visit to the lab, and the small drop of dried blood on the floor that greeted her. The imaginary suffering of her mother kept her company in that room. Eventually, her fa-ther brought her home to her terrified siblings. El-liot stopped asking her to find things.

As she grew older, she began to think more crit-ically about the possible consequences of her dis-ease. She remembered being forced to watch atomic weapon test footage. Farm animals tied to poles vaporized in a flash of light. Buildings turned to splinters by gusts of wind. The researchers showed her images of Hiroshima and Nagasaki victims, women with crackling, blackened skin, children with bulging tumors and distorted faces. They implored her to think about the weapon itself—to imagine it at her fingertips, on the table, beside her chair. They showed images of Fat Man and Little Boy, engineering diagrams she didn't understand. Exasperated, one of the researchers demanded that she bring them an atomic bomb. It had seemed laughably stupid at the time. She felt confident, looking at her father and his coworkers, waiting on her to deliver them a horrible weapon. She told them to just use the diagrams to build one themselves. "Can't you follow directions?" she had asked with heavy snark. But then the men started cutting her, and nothing was funny anymore.

Despite their ruthless ingenuity, Lise never brought them their prize. Her skin bore the scars of their attempts, but in that instance, her body hadn't betrayed her. Lately she wondered if her mom had succeeded, or thought she might succeed, at bringing over such a weapon. Or maybe her mom was tired of being cut, tired that her own imagination could betray her.

This thing inside her wasn't a gift or a superpower. It wasn't an illness, exactly. It was a monster made of fear, a powerful darkness built to conjure what it wanted. It had killed her mother and moved to a new victim. Now Lise kept it locked inside herself. She tried to study it, to understand, but that didn't keep her going. As long as she remained alive, it would spare Elliot and Sophie. So she lived, alone and with no other purpose than to live, to keep those she loved safe.

Lise retrieved a pillow from her armchair. Hesitating for a moment, she pulled down the photo of her mother and set it on the floor beside her. Covered up in a thin blanket next to the fire, her home enveloped in darkness, Lise felt as safe as she could feel.

6

―――――――――――――

NOVEMBER 10, 2003

5:45 PM

JULIE CAME BACK FROM THE FOOD COURT WITH Hostess cupcakes and coffee for the team. They had data to review and none of them had social lives. She felt maternal getting food and drinks for the team, yet her primary motive was selfish. She needed this walk. She took a longer route, breathing in the chilly fall air and the smell of dead leaves.

The breezeways between the classrooms and the research departments were silent. Some of the buildings had only a few windows illuminated. Street lights were casting their dingy yellow light across the gray and brown landscape. Students laughed to one another, shared stories from class, went in search of something other than ramen for dinner. Some had an air of crisp laziness that could only come from a steady stream of funds from home. Others wore their exhaustion with dignity, moving in haste from class to work, the promise of a few hours of sleep their daily reward.

Julie thought of all the money that had gone into Gordon while some of these students were struggling to eat. The occasional hunger she recalled from her own youth had been too sharp to glorify. Had her research been successful, it would have been important. But what were the costs of this failure?

As she walked with the cupcakes and coffee, she tabulated the components. They bought gold foil on discount, but gold was gold. Custom circuit boards she had outsourced to save time. The Swiss laser-machined top inside the machine generated a finely tuned static field. The superconducting iron oxypnictide had been purchased for an unknown amount, and Marshall had looked sick for days afterward.

Even the lead shielding around Gordon's most sensitive equipment was not made from standard materials. It had been melted down from ancient Roman artifacts and shipped to them in a brick—a very expensive brick. The background radiation present in newly extracted lead ore is almost entirely depleted in Roman lead. Most of it came from pipes, but some from coins and decorations. The thought of melting down historical artifacts made Julie uncomfortable, but Allison had laughed. "We aren't Stanford. They probably gave us lead from sewage pipes."

Then there was the promethium. The recollection of that negotiation made Julie shake with anger. It was listed in the budget as simply a "donation from Stoneham University." Dr. John Fields, Marshall's boss, had been over the moon at her negotiating skills. Marshall's reaction was more subdued. Todd Durham was the head of Stoneham's materials research, a notorious misogynist and Julie's ex-boyfriend from undergrad. She had never told Marshall why they had split up, but he seemed to know enough. The disgusting smirk on Todd's face when she asked for promethium haunted her.

Julie shook her head as she walked. That was all over now, she reminded herself, but it didn't feel over. It would never feel over. Years had passed since their last argument. The topic hadn't been love, or school, or money. She'd brought burritos back to his dorm for a study session, and he accused of her intentionally ordering onions on his. Julie looked at him in his ratty pajama pants as he self-righteously pointed at her with a foil-wrapped burrito, his face red with anger, and she'd let out one laugh. Todd struck her over the head with a closed fist. She still remembered the blurred close-up of his grimy floor as she lay stunned, the smell of Mexican food still fresh in the air. How had she landed there over something so stupid? In that moment, her life pivoted.

A part of her knew she would have stayed with Todd if things had been slightly different. One fewer kind smile from her father, maybe, or even a slight tweak in her neurochemistry, and she would have accepted his caresses, his tearful apology, and put up with his abuse again and again. She would have had kids, because he wanted kids, and would have kept a house with a white picket fence, because he wanted a housewife, and that would've been it for her. She didn't accept it, though. She was here now. With her own lab, her own condo, and her own TV. And an expensive teleportation machine that didn't work.

Julie reached the lab door and stared at the drawing of the box, noting lines that weren't quite straight and a smudged fingerprint. She sighed and pushed open the door, then paused for a moment on the threshold, registering Marshall's presence at Spencer's computer. He hadn't come by after their other failed attempts. Wary, she chose to ignore him. She stepped around Xiulan, who was putting away the laser scanner. Clearly, the sweep of Gordon's platform for any remnants of apple had failed. Julie sighed again and set the cupcakes and coffee down, checking which cup was Spencer's tea before bringing it to him.

"I guess no luck this time, eh, Julie?" Marshall said, looking away from the younger man's screen.

"Not this time," she muttered as she grabbed her own coffee and retreated to her workstation. She saw Xiulan and Allison exchange a meaningful glance.

"You need help looking at the data?" Marshall offered.

"We failed. What's to see."

"Thank you, Dr. Corrigan," Allison said quietly.

Marshall nodded and looked over at Gordon. "Maybe you guys should power him off. He's a massive energy hog."

Xiulan and Allison murmured their agreement and Spencer grunted noncommittally, but Julie said nothing. Her blue glasses askew, she rubbed her temples.

Marshall remained motionless for a moment, probably watching her, then left the room. The sounds of typing died out, a chair squeaked, and no one spoke.

"I can hear your eyes. Shut up," Julie commanded. The sounds of typing resumed. Allison put on her headphones, the miniature voices audible across the room. Julie heard Xiulan open her jar of neon foam earplugs.

Her mentor in grad school had told her not to be too ambitious. Accomplish smaller tasks, build from there, then set out to achieve something great. Julie knew he was right, but ignored him anyway. Now she felt the pain of her naivety. She'd always believed that if you aim high and miss, you'll still reach something important. Now that seemed incredibly childish. The experiment had failed. No incremental achievement had been made. The apple was untouched. Nothing had reached the landing platform. Alice wanted nothing to do with Bob or his ilk.

"Dr. Coyne, we've divided up the pages

equally. When you're ready, you start on page twenty-two."

"Fine, fine." She shoved her glasses back onto her face and slumped into her chair. She jerked her mouse to clear the screensaver and scanned for the output folder on the shared hard drive. Her hand stopped as her brain caught up. "Page twenty-two?"

Spencer turned back to his computer.

"We only had four or five pages last time, but I was new then . . . ," Xiulan said.

"Let's not get our hopes up," Julie said. "It's probably some glitch. Duplication error or something."

"Yeah, I . . . hmm." Spencer's words were lost as his fingers clicked on his keyboard. He shifted his chair closer, leaning toward the screen.

"What's up?" Allison had muted her headphones and was looking from one person to another. She bit into a Hostess cupcake.

"Ally, can you bring up Gordon's terminal?" Spencer asked.

Allison typed delicately with one unfrosted hand and loaded the black screen with her customized neon-pink characters. "Huh. What're you running, Spence? Doesn't look like our standard diagnostic," she said.

"I'm not running anything."

Allison put down the cupcake and wiped her hand on her jeans while looking at the same data on Xiulan's console. Allison returned to her console and entered a few commands. She tilted her head as she read the short list of names of her coworkers. As she typed in a new query, Xiulan peered over her shoulder.

"What are you checking for?" Xiulan asked.

"Active-user list for the program. Maybe a VPN connection."

"I checked for that already. Maybe it's a time-delayed script," Xiulan muttered, rolling back to her console to review the program's connection history.

"Well, this data has to be coming from some-where. Gordon isn't doing anything here."

Julie looked across the room at the work sta-tions and watched information populate the scien-tists' screens in perfect synchronicity. She felt more anxiety than excitement. Her creation was doing something unexpected, something inexplicable—something beyond her control.

"Okay. The experiment failed, right?" Xiulan asked, jabbing her finger at the apple. Spencer turned in his chair, quietly staring at it with Xiulan. No one responded. "So, guys? What the shit?"

7

FEBRUARY 26, 2013

5:04 PM

DANIEL WAS SETTING UP A HIGH-END LAPTOP, frowning as he worked. It had been traded in for lamps and a DVD player. Uncle Joe shrugged when Daniel asked if he could have it for school. Joe didn't seem to believe him, and he smiled as if he got his nephew's inner thoughts, but he was wrong. Daniel had a deep discomfort with technology. He wiped and reformatted the hard drive, bought antivirus software, checked the system for weird background programs and high CPU processes. Even when he finished and everything seemed okay, he still looked at the laptop with suspicion.

His anxiety wasn't misplaced. Most of the laptops they received were stolen. Sellers in shabby clothes who wouldn't, or couldn't, share the device's password were a strong clue. Neither he nor his uncle ever discussed the origins of the pawn shop's items, but it was safe to assume almost everything came from thieves. Some items were brought in by drug dealers who had been paid in belongings by desperate junkies. Uncle Joe handled those guys. Eventually the junkies came in, when they no longer had anything of value and had evolved into thieves themselves.

These experiences made Daniel unwilling to own the items in his uncle's shop, but the laptop was an exception. He did need it for school. One of his classes required software that was not available in the computer lab. The professors assumed everyone had at least a desktop at home, if not a laptop. For Daniel, who rarely went a month without being mugged, it was impossible to imagine a life in which you could bring your laptop to and from school.

With these facts in mind, he was willing to take this laptop and not pity whoever had owned it before him.

He found Q-tips and a small jar of plastic cleaner. He started scrubbing the faint brown residue from the keyboard. The space bar was particularly gross. He grabbed a fresh Q-tip and went back over the keyboard again, then cleaned the screen with a cloth and found a small scratch he could not repair. He sighed and applied a piece of fresh tape to the built-in webcam.

"Hi," a soft voice said.

Daniel almost jumped, his mind leaping to the ghost. A girl, probably about his age, shifted nervously beyond the glass and metal screen. She looked nice, though thin and haggard. He pushed the laptop aside and tried to hide the guilt he felt as her eyes followed it.

"Hi. How can I help you?"

The young woman smiled in embarrassment and took a little envelope of jewelry from her worn purse. "I was wondering how much I could get for these."

Daniel felt his stomach sink. Jewelry was his uncle's big-ticket item. They only paid for the weight of the gold or silver, but Uncle Joe turned around and sold the pieces to jewelry stores for a large profit. Daniel took the jewelry scale from a drawer as the girl slid the envelope through the window. Daniel gently removed the items one by one. There was a necklace with a cross pendant. A bracelet that looked like fake gold. A string of pearls. A large, beautiful ring with onyx and dia-monds that was probably worth thousands.

He weighed each item with delicate respect and filled out the slip. The fake gold bracelet he set aside. After the government brought down pan-demic houses and seized property, bits of jewelry were often all that was left to the survivors. Only the wealthy could justify owning something so useless anymore.

"This place feels loved," she observed with a quiet smile.

Daniel's thoughts stuttered. He looked up, fol-lowing her gaze. The contrast of her words and his thoughts required examination. The metal grates protecting the office were gray, rust speckled where the paint had chipped. The bullet-resistant windows were papered over, the daylight coming through tinged a menacing red-brown. The light was harsh in the office, dim in the store itself, neither area welcoming or warm. She laughed softly, letting her gaze fall over the abandoned objects on the shelves. "Maybe not the place, then."

He pulled over the calculator and added up the total. One by one, he placed the items back into her envelope. Optimistically, he slid her both the envelope and the slip of paper.

She looked at the total, tears welling in her eyes. With another sad smile, she nodded and said, "Hey, at least I get to keep the bracelet!"

Daniel tried to return her smile and failed. The young woman slid the envelope back toward him. The bracelet she tucked back into her purse. As she walked out of the store with her cash, he added the items in with the other unsorted jewelry. The squeaking fan in the corner grew louder in the silence she left behind. The smell of his leftover breakfast wafted upwards from the trash can. *Could she have smelt that? What about me? I haven't even showered today.*

His last Q-tip had dried. He had planned to clean out the ports on the sides of the laptop, but the cotton tip was dingy. If he reused that end, he'd just swirl around more dirt. He put away the cleaning supplies and sat still for several moments, staring at empty doorway. He had homework he could do, soon. Not quite yet.

Daniel pushed back from the desk. He grabbed a cup from the water cooler, filled it with ice water, and drank it so quickly it hurt his throat. He pushed open the metal office door, walked through the shop to the front door, and locked it. He shut off the lights in the shop. It was basically closing time anyway.

He surveyed the aisles in the dim light from the office windows and thought of the girl's words. Some of these things had been loved. A purple glass lamp called to him. When the guy selling the laptop was looking at lamps, Daniel noticed this one had a signature on it that Uncle Joe had over-looked. The guy chose two carved lamps, their bases a matching pair of portly cross-eyed lions. The signed one had been deposited on the wrong shelf. Daniel walked over to the lamp, crouching to examine it. He picked it up, rubbing his thumb across the signature. Carefully, he brought it through the metal door and placed it next to the new laptop. He opened a browser window and searched for lost-and-found listings.

Several hours later, he had a small pile of belongings on the desk, each tagged with their original owner's information. An inscribed pocket watch was set aside. He had found articles in the local paper, as well as a Craigslist post, explaining that it was stolen during a home invasion. The widow and children of the owner were offering a reward. He didn't feel confident contacting the person who posted the ad, but he found the family's address. He set the other objects out of sight. With bus fare in the pocket without the hole and the pocket watch hidden in his waistband, he was ready to go.

The express bus slid through the city streets. The interior was filled with yellow light, illuminating the typical early-evening crowd passing from the better part of downtown through the grimy streets to the suburbs. Tired businessmen and –women kept their eyes down. Daniel averted his eyes from teenagers too awkward for their high heels and hoop earrings. Young men bobbed their heads to loud, distorted music on their smartphones. A lady with a dog in a purse, a child in a school uniform and a backpack who looked too young to be out alone, an old man carrying an umbrella even though it was a sunny day. There was a little old lady whose lap was concealed by more red plastic shopping bags than anyone could ever need. Nearly all of them were wearing white masks, except for Daniel, one of the teenagers, and the child.

Daniel's stop approached. He pulled the cord and disembarked. Two of the teenagers got off, their shrill laughter echoing down the street as they walked away. The old man with the umbrella strolled ahead until he turned off the main street. Daniel checked the address and walked nervously down the unfamiliar suburban thoroughfare. After a few blocks, he found the street he was looking for.

Large Victorian houses stood proudly behind the blossoming cherry trees. Imperfect rectangles of green grass peeked through boundaries of decorative fencing. A quaint little house with wide columns and painted shingles on the side had a Valentine's Day flag fluttering in the breeze. The sidewalks were old, the curbs almost flat against the road. In some places cobblestones peeped through worn patches of asphalt, the only signs of decay in this neighborhood.

Daniel remembered looking at open houses around here with his parents. They had never been able to afford one, but they would look from time to time, sighing about the shorter commute and the better school district. His dad would say, "Maybe when they open up that new processing center, I'll make manager," and his mom would agree, and say, "Once I'm done with my master's degree." But Daniel was happy in their boring little house. He had never wanted change.

Interspersed with the stately homes were vacant lots; the houses that were demolished during the pandemic were only memories now. There had been rumors that the contagion was absorbed by porous surfaces and could linger dormant in walls and floorboards for years, even decades. The state capital was almost burned to the ground years ago. Maniacs in pickups loaded with kerosene and propane blew up or set fire to every building they could reach until they were killed by police. What had happened here, though, was not a mob, but bureaucracy. City council had voted to demolish the homes where more than one infected person had died. Daniel looked around at the rows of untouched houses, recalling entire blocks that were demolished downtown. He doubted the rule had been enforced uniformly.

He had been walking for ten minutes, trying to act casual as he examined the numbers. The house he wanted he nearly passed by, until he noticed the spray-painted number on the sidewalk. As deftly as he could, he crept up the wooden steps to the porch and left the pocket watch on the welcome mat. He took a big breath. With a jab, he rang the doorbell, then ran, speeding down the sidewalk until he was sure he was out of sight.

Once back on the thoroughfare, he smiled, unable and unwilling to conceal how good he felt. Finally, he was doing the right thing.

8

DECEMBER 16, 2020

10:22 AM

LISE'S BACKPACK WAS FULL. THE BURNERS WERE ALL off, she had closed up all the windows and doors, and her generator was unplugged. She planned to return to her little house soon, but every trip to the internet café was risky. She had to be ready to make a quick escape. In the bag was everything that was important to her: her mother's photograph, two of each type of tea, her favorite mug, some clothes, a lockpick set, and all of her money. She double checked that the ladder was nowhere near the panel in the ceiling. The weapons she left behind.

The cold air was brisk. Lise had spent so much time indoors that she was too weak to complete the walk without resting. The journey involved descending forested hillsides to the highway, crossing the highway, then walking down the small street that served as downtown to the few thousand people who inhabited the region. The distance was only a couple of miles, but she would need at least two breaks. She ignored the trembling in her knees and enjoyed the view from the trail.

The tall trees, each individually beautiful, lived together in tight clusters, covering the rolling hills in a prickly blanket of green. Deep in the valleys, mist formed and floated like a dragon hidden beneath the forest canopy. Despite the mist, the sky was clear enough that she could see the top of Longs Peak more than thirty miles away. For the third year in a row, it was a bare and gray jagged ridge in the sky. No snow.

She rested at a fallen tree and mechanically ate a protein bar. The soft moss cushioning her fingers called her attention. Droplets of dew still clung to the twisted verdant strands that each curled and reached in a different direction. Every little piece was delicate and beautiful. She wondered how many living things, lovely and ambitious, she hadn't noticed in her walk. She decided to look up the life cycle of moss at the café. *It would be great to just pull up the information on a phone.* With sharp alarm, she pushed the desire aside.

Brushing crumbs from her hands and dirt off the seat of her jeans, Lise hiked the backpack up onto her shoulders. She gave a parting glance to the little patch of moss, then continued down the hill. After a short walk and one more rest, she arrived at the road and nature gave way to pavement. She kept her distance, trudging through the grass and shrubs littered with plastic cups, papers, diapers, and worse. Cars flew past, honking at each other in frustration. She didn't understand why.

Soon the small group of storefronts came into view. The yellow sign above the Chinese restaurant had faded to near white. Across stood a truck stop, a foreboding place she always avoided. There was a vacuum and appliance repair store with heavy mesh wire over the windows, a dingy but busy post office, an abandoned ski shop, and the bright, clean, and relatively new internet café—her destination. She kept her head down and pushed open the door.

Lise reached the counter and ordered a hot chocolate. Under the pretense of rummaging through her backpack, she obscured her face and retreated to her favorite computer. Though the café was unusually busy, her station was empty. Crammed into a corner by the kitchen door with barely enough legroom, the spot was uncomfortable and noisy, but it had easy access to a rear exit and was backed against a wall, which provided extra privacy. A post behind the monitor blocked her from the security camera in the far corner.

Lise pushed the webcam askew before sitting down. Hesitatingly, she opened a new tab and typed from memory a long, complicated URL. A 505 Error page. She clicked on an invisible button in the corner and a password-request box appeared. She entered an 18-character password.

Inside was an encoded message from Kee, her

friend from high school. She knew the code by heart now but needed scratch paper for some of the deciphering work.

Kee was working as a software engineer in San Jose, and his intelligence, skill, and paranoia made him the only person she trusted. Even with his precautions, she knew any connection to technology invited danger. Movement in her peripheral vision startled her, but it was just the barista with her hot chocolate. Taking a sip, Lise noticed a young man with rumpled clothes walk in. He scanned the faces of the patrons while he bit his lip. She returned to Kee's email. She had asked for help finding someone, and he had finally gotten back to her with his address. She scribbled it down on a piece of paper and stuffed it into her pocket.

Kee was her only friend paranoid enough to believe her about her dad's experiments. Lise never went into detail about what she could do, but Kee seemed to have some idea. They were close before her dad pulled her out of school, and then he became her only connection outside of her family.

The night she left home, she visited Kee's house on the pretense of walking the dog. Lise was not allowed to have friends, so she regularly used her stepmother's lapdog as an excuse to get away. After an hour listening to spoilers about the graphic novel she was borrowing, Lise left Kee and shambled back to her family's immaculate Queen Anne home. The branches of the cherry trees were gnarled fingers stretching over the sidewalk as the dog sniffed at refuse caught in the cobblestone street. Lise slowed when the house came into view. Her stepmother's car wasn't in the driveway, but her father's was still there. Quietly, she ascended the porch and entered through the back door. Her brother and sister's tiny shoes were missing from the mudroom; her father's socks carelessly awaited her stepmother's attention.

Lise unleashed the dog and let him in first. He didn't immediately run across the house as he usually did. He paced in the kitchen, sniffing the air and the ground. Lise held his leash in a limp hand, her eyes following the bloody footprints that crisscrossed the floor.

Her voice was hoarse as she called out for her dad. The kitchen, dining room, hallway, and foyer were empty. In the small downstairs office she found him. Papers strewn across the floor. Her father's face, a face she hated, was disfigured and bulging from the blows that killed him. Lise stood frozen as the world grew dim and hollow. She was still carrying the dog's leash when she vomited in the bathroom. There were tears in her eyes, not of remorse, but of what? She didn't know. When she heard a sound upstairs, she ran through the house in panic, slipping on her father's blood. She grabbed his phone, wallet, and keys from the counter and rushed outside. With trembling fingers, she called her stepmother.

"Hey hon . . ."

Lise cut her off. "Don't . . . Don't bring the kids home. Call the police."

"Lise, what . . ."

"Dad is dead. I think they are still in the house." Lise began to cry.

"Oh my God. How could you—your own father."

Lise held back a sob. *Of course they'd suspect me. They'll convict me, make me disappear and cut me open.*

"Tell Sophie and Elliot I love them. I'll always love them."

Hours later she was hiding in the bushes at Kee's house with no memory of the journey there. Surrounded by the tangy smell of leaves and bark, she realized she could never go home. She replayed the scenes over and over. Who could have done it? Could there have been a motive other than herself? Drugs, money, and affairs—

He wasn't the type to trust drugs. He made money from the government for access to her, but was there other money, even bloodier money at stake? Had he had an affair? Unlikely. It was Lise's illness. Her only happiness was her siblings, and they had been taken from her. This disease ruined everything.

Nearly an hour passed before she was brave enough to surface. Clumsily sneaking to the spot under Kee's window, she knocked on the glass, startling her friend.

At a glance, he saw something terrible had happened. He composed himself and helped her climb inside. Though only seventeen, he'd spent most of his life planning an escape from the government; he knew Lise would need his help when the time came. He had always told her to come to him if things turned bad with her dad. Now he helped her without hesitation.

He snuck her into his parents' house, took the wallet and keys from her. He shut the curtains, turned off his wireless router, removed the battery from his smartphone, and sorted through her belongings. He saw the vomit on her clothes and wordlessly guided her to the bathroom, turned on the shower, and left her alone.

She returned slightly cleaner to find her father's work badge and car-key fob in pieces. While she changed into the clean clothes Kee set out for her, Kee sat at his worktable cutting open the wallet. He seemed surprised not to find any tracking equipment. Still, he put most of the components into a glass bowl and destroyed them in his kitchen microwave.

When he finally spoke, he asked about her siblings. "They'll be safe with Helen." He didn't bring them up again.

Before they left his house, he set up a new email account for her. Lending her his brother's bike, he went with her to withdraw cash from her dad's bank account. He left her in the darkness of an adjacent parking lot, then concealed himself in an oversized hoodie and sunglasses. He strolled up with a distinctive yet unrecognizable walk, withdrew cash, and returned to her with an overstuffed envelope. The disguise abandoned, they peddled to the bus station together, where he handed her a small notebook.

"This is for decrypting the cypher we'll use until I figure out how we can communicate over the internet. Wait two months, at least, then send me a postcard with an address for an abandoned building at least a mile away from where you settle down. I'll send instructions from there. If you ever lose contact with me, I'll leave money and instructions at the tree where Kyle Crosswhite kicked Andy Byer in the nuts after we got back from science camp. Don't call anyone, don't use a computer, keep your head down and hoodie up." As they stood together in the white light of the bus station lights, Lise looked at the bikes.

"How are you going to get both of these home?"

Kee shook his head. Without another word, he gave her a hug, the last physical contact she would share with anyone for five years.

Lise sat alone in the café thinking of their goodbye. Kee had probably forgotten the importance of that hug.

Since then, he had helped her take money from her father's secret bank accounts. He funneled the funds into nondescript offshore accounts she could access and programmed the transfers to look pedestrian. Paychecks from a major payroll company, tax refunds, the sorts of transfers people normally receive. From there, some of her money was deposited in small amounts as checks to a bank account in someone else's name. She took quarterly trips to different cities, withdrew cash, then never went to that city again. Kee monitored the account and let her know if anything looked suspicious. Lise wasn't sure how he did it, but it wasn't legal. Sometimes she got the sense that he enjoyed the work precisely because he didn't profit from it. She finished checking her accounts, closed her tabs, cleared the browser history, and decided to look up information about moss.

The screen flickered. It had never done that before. Lise frowned. She looked around. No one seemed to be acting strange. The young man from earlier still seemed like he was looking for someone, which was unusual. She turned back to her computer, touching nothing. It could've just been her vision acting up¾ an eyelash or something, maybe. She watched it as her suspicion grew and then began to abate. Then one of the cooling fans kicked on in the tower at her feet.

Something's wrong.

She gathered her things and left the café.

The air felt colder now. The crisp sensation stung her skin. Clouds were building overhead, and they swam in her vision as angry tears welled in her eyes. *I've been careless.* She pushed her anger aside and pulled her backpack straps tighter on her shoulders. Perhaps, rather than find a new hiding place, she could do something different. Kee had given her the address to someone she very much wanted to speak to. She began the hike to the bus station.

9

NOVEMBER 10, 2003

6:25 PM

JULIE THANKED THE CALLER AND HUNG UP. SHE WAS interrupted from writing her notes by Allison's brisk steps. The graduate student was out of breath as she marched into the lab.

"I just asked everyone who is still here for the day. JT says they've been getting weird results in his undergrad class's cavity QED trials. Where's the radio?"

Julie didn't look up from her terminal. "Anything else?"

"Someone in the bio department complained they were getting interference during a proton-exchanger experiment. Do you guys know where a radio is? A Walkman, boombox, whatever. Or the emergency radio? It wasn't in the earthquake kit."

Xiulan helped Allison find the radio as Julie and Spencer glared at their screens, typing, copying, and pasting. Julie brought up her email and entered keywords until she had found every message from her friends and associates who were working on teleportation. She pulled up a map of the United States and began to write down coordinates for their research facilities and universities.

"Did you talk to Avery?" Julie asked over her shoulder. No one responded, so she kept working. She heard static and Allison and Xiulan's voices fading as they walked down the hall. When her list of coordinates was complete, she entered them into the plaintext file she had pulled of Gordon's data. None was a match.

Static suddenly filled the room. Julie turned in confusion. The women had apparently been wandering the halls with the radio. They changed the dial but the static continued.

"That is incredibly distracting," Spencer muttered, but Julie was focused on Allison's face.

Allison looked at the device with muted terror. "All the radios in the building are doing this. We walked all the way out to the security desk. They said their radio cut out at around 3:30. Three minutes after we powered on Gordon."

Julie frowned. While her assistants discussed who was capable of this type of prank, she grabbed a pin from a small tool chest and placed it on a table near Gordon. It didn't move. She placed it closer to Gordon. Still nothing. She returned it to the tool chest. The static on the radio continued.

"What about Farheen? He's running that thing in the gravity lab. Anything from him?"

"He was out today. He wouldn't do this," Allison replied as she turned off the radio.

"I don't even know how anyone could pull this off," Spencer observed.

"Do you guys see a pattern here? I think I do but I'm not sure," Xiulan asked from her console.

"I thought I saw something," Spencer replied, turning back to his screen. "You wanna put together a chart or should I?"

"I've got it," Xiulan responded, her screen already filled with a spreadsheet.

A phone rang somewhere in the building, but it was ignored. Julie moved over to the transport pad, her face a mask of suppressed anxiety. This was their fourth attempt at running Gordon. She had been growing desperate for him to do something, anything, to validate their effort. Now he was doing something. They had given the machine a name, and now he had a purpose. But it wasn't the one he had been programmed with, and that was remarkably frightening.

When the first phone stopped ringing, the lab phone began to ring. Allison answered it, spoke quietly for a moment, then covered the receiver as she tapped Julie on the shoulder.

"What?"

"It's maintenance. They said . . . I guess the building's water pressure is too high. They want us to back up our data and leave in case there is a rupture."

Julie sighed. "Okay, go ahead and make sure everything is saved, but don't power down. I'll be right back."

She put her hair into a ponytail and walked out of the lab to Marshall's office.

He was sitting at his desk reviewing papers that had once been arranged in neat piles. Now the order, if it existed, was one only he could decipher.

"What's up, Jules?"

"I was wondering if you heard about the water pressure?"

"Yeah, but they've said that a few times the past couple months. We didn't flood then; I doubt we will now. You guys should go. Gordon's not going to do anything tonight."

"A few times?"

"Yeah, weren't you here last time? I think you were running a trial, actually. I had to help find a plumber. Anyway, it's not a big deal." When she didn't respond, Marshall looked up from his writing. Something about her expression made him set down his pen and prepare to rise from his seat. Julie sat down quickly to stop him.

"What's wrong?"

"We've got data coming in."

Marshall leaned in. "Data is good. Any apple movement?"

"Not the apple. Not anything else that we can see or measure directly. There's been some interference reported throughout the physics wing. Nothing major. And . . . do you have a radio in here?"

When he shook his head no, Julie shrugged and continued. "We're getting static on the radio in the building. I'm not sure how far we need to go from Gordon for it to stop. Maybe we should map that. If the distance isn't noteworthy, perhaps the materials that block or reduce it might be. Anyway, it reaches at least to the security desk. I think there are campus maps in the cafeteria we could use."

"Hold on, Julie. So you think Gordon is transmitting?"

"I'm not sure," she admitted. "He's doing something. The data looks like what we would expect if he was moving things we told him to, but there are some peculiarities."

"Such as?"

"We aren't seeing anything move. The high volume of calls and the short intervals between transmissions. It's about an object every three seconds, but sometimes the pauses are smaller or greater. We were only expecting to have one transmission—the apple from one place to another. There would've been the time and location of departure and time and location of arrival in the log. Right now, it's showing THOUSANDS of entries."

"Okay."

"The entries aren't the same output we programmed into the software. There is unfamiliar code with the transmissions, alongside coordinates. I think it's a location modifier of some kind, but it changed to another code just recently. There have only been two of these codes so far."

"Individual machines, you think? Like recipients?"

Julie shrugged. "That might make sense. The coordinates between the two identifiers overlapped in Palo Alto, immediately before the first one disappeared and immediately after the new one appeared. Coordinates for ID 2 are now someplace else. An empty plot of land in the middle of nowhere in Colorado."

"Weird."

"I thought I had a lead at one point. A whole group, very early in the transmission, was at Stoneham University on the East Coast. The second ID was there for a couple of blips. You remember Todd, he and I used to . . . well, he was in our thermo lab?"

The name caused a cloud to fall across Marshall's face. He nodded.

"I gave him a call. He hasn't reported any strange activity. No appearances or disappearances, no radio static, either."

"This sounds like a prank."

Julie nodded slowly. "It must be, I guess. A very elaborate prank. It requires detailed knowledge of our experiment and editing of our software. Not many people have access."

Marshall got up, unrolled his shirtsleeves and walked to her lab. Julie followed. A flyer on a corkboard near the hallway water fountain caught her eye: *Buried under clutter? Join us for a campus-wide 'garage sale.'*

As they entered the lab, the three assistants

were gathered around Allison's console, staring at the screen.

"What now?" Julie asked.

"Allison figured out what one of the codes represents," Spencer said, unable to conceal his admiration.

"It's not that big of a deal," the young researcher replied with a blush. "I used to work at a store over summer break. It wasn't a store, really, it was a big warehouse distribution center. I can't stand actual customers. Anyway, the company used this same numerical taxonomy. They call them PLU codes. It must be pretty popular for it to turn up here. Each item has an ID number. It starts with a category identifier, then this is the subcategory, if there is one, then the item. I got to the point where I almost had them memorized back then. So this one, 2218437, is the full ID number, right?"

No one responded as Allison used her keyboard to switch to her browser screen. "Here's a full taxonomy of this ID system. 221 is the main category, which we keep seeing over and over in the records. 84 is the subcategory, and 37 is the item."

Allison entered a command to search the page for the ID number.

"Does that say . . . shotgun?" Marshall asked in a quiet voice.

Xiulan responded in a hushed voice. "221 is a weapons category."

10

MARCH 11, 2013

9:15 AM

Daniel hadn't been looking forward to spring break. Most college students in the city got out of town on vacation. Some of his study-group friends pooled their money and drove to the beach, but Daniel used the opportunity to get in more hours at the pawn shop.

It wasn't simply a money-making maneuver. Something had been bothering Uncle Joe over the last few weeks, but he wasn't likely to tell Daniel. It might be related to lady friends; his heavyset, hairy uncle had a surprisingly large number of admirers. Rather than pry, Daniel minded his own business and hoped Joe would settle down with someone nice.

It was early on Monday when Daniel flipped on the lights in the office. The shop didn't open until ten, so he had time to research. Today he'd look into a wallet with an embroidered name, an expensive-looking doll, and an engagement ring. After setting up his laptop and grabbing a cup of water, Daniel started his search with an online classifieds service. There were many wallets listed, mostly plain ones lost by people still hopeful they'd get the contents back. Nothing matched the wallet on the desk.

He leaned back in his chair and examined it again. The wallet was empty but it felt expensive. The warm brown leather had faded to honey gold near the embroidery. The leather and stitching seemed good quality, and the name "Miguel" was surrounded by intricate floral motifs. Daniel sat forward again and launched an automated translator tool. He entered some keywords and returned to the classifieds website, changing the language from English to Spanish. He found descriptions of similar wallets, but nothing identical.

After another hour of searching English- and Spanish-language newspaper classifieds, Daniel heard the buzzer for the back door. His uncle had returned. Daniel suddenly realized he hadn't opened the shop at ten. He pushed aside the items he was looking up and minimized his search window.

"Danny," his uncle shouted, "you gotta open up the damn shop if you're going to come in early. That's the deal."

"Sorry, I'm sorry."

He flipped on the lights, checked that the aisles were in order, then turned the Closed sign to Open. He drew up the two curtains and unlocked the front door. No one was outside; it was unlikely they had missed any customers.

Daniel returned to the office, preparing to apologize again. His uncle was looking at the wallet in confusion.

"What's going on here?"

Daniel felt his ears redden. He didn't want to keep it a secret, but he didn't want to tell his uncle about it either. "Oh, I was just seeing if any of this stuff was mentioned online. If there were rewards or whatever. Could bring in more money than, you know, what we'd make selling it."

Uncle Joe considered this for a moment until a thought occurred to him. He shook his head violently. "No, Danny, no. Some of this stuff, it's . . . we can't do that. Just leave it on the shelves and keep a low profile. Got it? No more of this, okay? No more."

"But Joe, this stuff doesn't sell."

Joe rolled his eyes and gathered up the wallet, doll, and ring. "They don't want them to sell. They want the ghost to take them. Look, it's complicated. Stop asking questions."

The young man opened his mouth to argue, but closed it and nodded. Uncle Joe put the items into the box with the other things Daniel wanted to research. He carried them to the small safe, fumbling with his keys for a moment before he opened the metal door and placed the box inside.

"Why don't you work on some homework, Danny, until customers come in. You cleaned up the place real good yesterday. There isn't anything that needs doin' now."

Daniel smiled weakly and nodded, sitting at the desk with his laptop, bringing up the school's website. There wasn't much homework to do, but he could start on next week's research paper. He put on his headphones, muffling the sounds of his uncle's heavy steps up to the apartment they shared above the shop. Daniel pulled up the digital library. His eyes glazed over. He took his headphones back off and walked around the shop. While he examined a porcelain figure of a child reaching for an apple in a tree, he heard a faint *pop*.

He stood, expecting to see that something had fallen. But there was nothing. The sound reminded him of the poppers kids used to buy from the ice cream truck. Turning the corner to another aisle, he saw that a knife was missing from a butcher block. It had been a complete set, he was almost sure of it. But now the largest slot in the wooden frame was empty. He pulled the block out to look behind it. He got on his knees to look on the floor. He checked nearby shelves in case it had landed there by some freak geological shudder. The knife was gone, as if it had never existed. Daniel stood, momentarily too frightened to move. Forcing himself forward, he returned to the caged office, sat at his laptop, and opened his school assignments, hoping they'd have customers soon.

• • •

A few days later, Daniel started early again and began restocking the shelves with new arrivals. The missing knife had been mostly forgotten, though he kept music playing over his laptop and every light flipped on when he was alone in the building.

Daniel heard the buzzer, and soon after, his uncle appeared. Rather than taking his normal route to the stairs, Joe walked briskly to the desk where they kept money and jewelry. He was sweating and looked angry. He had early meetings sometimes, but they were mysterious and clearly not intended for Daniel. It seemed to him that pawn shop owners keep rough company.

While his uncle rummaged around in a cabinet behind the counter, Daniel called out, "Hey, Joe, the ghost took another gun from the cabinet this morning. I was thinking, maybe we should try tying a string to them, and maybe tie the string to the backing board in the cabinet. I'd even want to put a bell on it, just to see what happens."

"Sure, sounds fun," Joe replied. Daniel furrowed his brow. He thought through the process of securing the guns as his uncle continued to search for something.

After a few moments, Daniel called out, "Do you need help?"

"No, no, I'm fine."

Daniel continued to write labels for the items he was stocking. Seconds later, Joe called from the back office, "Shit, dammit. Danny, I don't see a sales slip for that pocket watch we had a few months back. Do you remember the one I mean? With the really long chain?"

Daniel swallowed and said, "Doesn't ring a bell." He continued to put things on the shelves, his handwriting on the price tags not as precise as it was moments earlier.

He thought of the curtains of that suburban home fluttering open after he dropped off the pocket watch. He thought of how proud he'd felt returning stolen goods. He had stolen from his uncle, in a way. It didn't seem like there was a perfect right and wrong in that situation.

"It's not the kind of thing the ghost would take," Joe said to himself.

Daniel kept shuffling items to the shelves, occasionally pretending to examine them. He felt the eyes of his uncle hit him.

"Danny, oh no. Danny."

He looked back over his shoulder. Uncle Joe was flushed, and his agitation had turned to concern and fear. He had never seen his uncle afraid before. "Where is the pocket watch. Did you take it? I won't be mad, just give it back to me right now, okay, pal?"

Daniel lowered his head in shame. "Uncle, I . . . I can't. I gave it away. To the owners. I saw a lost-and-found flyer, and, well, I just . . ."

His words died on his lips as he watched his uncle's face. The concern and fear turned to anger, then terror. Sweat that had been glistening on his brow now streamed down his face. His eyes were red with tears. "Jesus Christ, Danny. Jesus. What have you done? What have you done?"

Daniel's jaw dropped and his pulse quickened. He had never seen his uncle afraid before. The older man walked to Daniel, then fell to his knees and sat back on his heels, wiping his face and pulling at his hair. "Oh my God, oh God. Shit. Shit."

"We can just, can't we just say we lost it?" Daniel sat on the floor too, his voice small. Without warning, Joe leaned forward and slapped him in the face once, then twice.

In a whisper like a scream, he said, "They know now, don't you see? And it's our fault they know. It's our fault, because you . . . why did you, Danny? I took you in. Why?"

Tears filled Daniel's eyes; his face burned and swelled. "It was just a watch. What did I do?"

"They're going to kill me. They'll kill us both. Oh God, why did you do it?"

11

DECEMBER 19, 2020

9:04 PM

LISE DISEMBARKED FROM THE BUS BEFORE THE END OF her ticket. She'd purchase another in cash at a new station and continue on to her destination. They'd be keeping an eye out for her, but they would assume she'd use a car. They didn't know how her illness worked. They probably thought she could magic one into existence.

If she kept to quiet routes and changed her appearance, she could travel without too much trouble. Originally she had planned to dye her hair in a gas station restroom, but she had never done that before. The results might call too much attention to her. She wished she could disguise herself as a man, like she had after her family was killed.

She was getting tired. Fatigue made her clumsy, and she couldn't afford any mistakes. She found a van for sale on the side of the road, picked the lock and climbed inside. It didn't seem possible that they would look for her there, yet as she pushed away from the window and snuggled into the arch of the wheel well, she felt vulnerable.

Lise thought of all the things they would do to her if they found her. Her father had used them as her boogie man. Any minor infraction or wayward glare would invoke the question: "Do you want to go back to the lab?" It was a secret the two of them kept from her stepmother and siblings. Her step-mother saw the scars once. She didn't know what her husband did for a living, but she knew he wasn't a businessman. Lise had assumed their rela-tionship would make more sense when she was an adult. Now adulthood had arrived, and she real-ized the only answer was that Helen was weak. A natural dependent. Helen wasn't a stupid woman; she knew enough about what was going on that she could have done something. She should have done something.

Lise would never sleep if she didn't stop think-ing. She squeezed her eyes shut and imagined cleaning the floorboards at her little forest home. Scrubbing with a soft, soapy brush. Rinsing with a rag. Moving on. Coming back to the beginning with another clean rag, scooping up the hard pol-ish, pushing it into the grain, then wiping down the boards. When the shine was consistent, moving on to a new section. Scrubbing, rinsing, polishing, until the world faded away.

• • •

The next morning, Lise tied her shoes with extra care – she had to vary her methods of transportation, and today was a walking day. She packed her things quickly. She wanted to be away from the van before rush hour started. She pushed the soft, soapy brush underneath the front seat. Cautiously, she opened the rear door to examine her surroundings before setting off.

At the first bus stop, she examined a map of the city. There was a straight route to downtown. Judging by the illustrator's color scheme, it was a busy thoroughfare. The smaller streets connected to one another to make a route in the same direction. Lise wasn't sure which was safer; walking as a stranger in the midst of neighborhoods or on the side of a road that would be taken by anyone looking for her. In the end, her unreliable memory made her chose the busy road. To ease the tension in her gut, she decided to stick to the side of the street with the clearest escape routes.

The city was flat, brown, and quiet. It had the feeling of good times long gone. Lise walked by a strip mall. A row of smaller shops, boarded with plywood or simply left for squatters and a large anchor store at the center, itself dismantled years ago. She continued on, passing several blocks of a residential neighborhood until she arrived at another strip mall, designed at the same time in the same way. The walk took on the feeling of a stich she learned in home economics; long stretches terminated by a dot, beginning again in endless succession.

People lived in the middle spaces between the commercial intersections. The housing spaced in walking distance from the stores at each end, yet Lise saw no other pedestrians. The rectangles of yard around each housing development showcased every shade of landscaping gravel she could imagine. Tan, brown, black, burgundy. Concrete block walls in brown, beige, gray, sometimes with stucco, occasionally topped with decorative tiles or stones. The houses themselves were equally monotonous, the variety only in the degree of desperation reflected by their tenants.

After hours of walking, Lise approached the first set of stores that looked inhabited and approachable. Though it was only late morning, hot air shimmered off the nearly-vacant black parking lot.

Lise stopped at one that had a fast food restaurant. Wearing her baseball hat pushed down low, she ordered fries and a soda. She left with her lunch, examining the nail salon, smoke shop, and rundown pet store in the same stucco complex. Large fans were set up at the nail salon, the employees clustered in misery near the front door and looking out to the horizon, at nothing at all. Lise moved on.

A mile later, in a newer development with saplings anchored to large poles, she found a hair salon. After a quick conversation with the receptionist, Lise was guided to a chair. A hairdresser appeared from the back room, her conversation with a coworker interrupted by Lise's arrival. She snapped her gum as she flicked Lise's hair left, right, and forward. The woman asked what she wanted with disinterest. This was fine. Right now Lise had nothing to say and didn't want to be memorable.

The woman returned with gloves, a brush, and a plastic mixing bowl full of bleach. The solution stung Lise's scalp at first, then began to itch. It was hard to resist the urge to scratch. As the brush moved across sections of her head, Lise stared at a bumper sticker on another stylist's mirror: "I'm a beautician, not a magician!"

Once Lise's hair was coated in white, the stylist rolled a large heater behind her chair. It looked like a robotic assassin in the mirror. Its enormous round heating elements glowed like insect eyes examining her scalp with unwavering scrutiny. Lise relaxed and tried to imagine she was like the other women in the salon. Doing something for herself. Improving her confidence.

The stylist returned long after the timed heater had shut off, her eyes puffy as she placed her cell phone in a pocket. A sympathetic look was all Lise could offer to her. The woman nodded and forced out a small smile. She seemed to appreciate not being asked what had happened.

The stylist guided Lise to a washing station and scrubbed out the bleach. After her hair turned a pale straw color, Lise returned to her original chair and watched the stylist mix bright dye in a plastic container. The stylist asked, "You have any kids?"

"No." The silence that followed implied that one word was insufficient, so she followed up. "I probably never will."

"Let me tell you, they can be your greatest joy or your greatest mistake."

Lise swallowed hard, feeling herself in treacherous emotional waters.

"Most of the time, they are worth it. Just not today. Why don't you want to have kids?"

"Got a genetic thing from my mom. I don't want to pass it down."

"Hmm. Most people 'round here would say something about God having a plan for you. I won't. If I'm living God's plan, well. He knows just what I think of Him."

Lise closed her eyes. Her social skills suffered from disuse.

"Ho-ly shi-t, honey! Your neck."

Lise opened her eyes slowly, exchanging a look in the mirror with the hairdresser. "My dad was abusive."

"Mine too, but sweetheart, wow. These are bad. He must have been a goddamned animal. Did you ever call the cops on him?"

"He was sort of a big shot. And I didn't want my brother and sister to end up in CPS."

The woman nodded knowingly as she leaned over to whisper, pointing her dye brush for emphasis. "See, that is the problem with the system. If you're a smart kid, you don't report it. You'll just see your family broken up or you get lucky and you all end up with some shitbag child molester. Well, I hope he got what was coming to him."

"He did."

Lise looked down at the trash can at her feet, begging herself not to finish the thought.

The stylist patted Lise's shoulder and gave it a squeeze.

A few hours later, she looked at the slip and counted out her cash.

"Here's my business card. Got them printed up at the office supply place last week. I kinda like them."

Lise smiled and nodded at the card, staring at the printed name. The stylist looked at her with confusion.

"Sorry. Julie was my mother's name."

The stylist gave her a firm hug, kissed the top of her head and whispered, "You take care of yourself now, sweet pea. Wish you were my own little girl."

It was late at night when Lise boarded a new bus. Her new hat, heavy eyeliner, lightened eyebrows, light red hair and black clothes made her look strange to herself. People seemed to take no notice of her. She chose a window seat and leaned her forehead on the glass, looking out at the fluorescent-hued landscape. She'd take this bus to a stop before her ticket ran out, then make one last transfer. There was someone she wanted to see.

She had thought about moving to a new, quiet location. Laying low, researching, then maybe finding someone who could cure her, or at least had answers for her and wouldn't hurt her. Looking at her strange new reflection in the window, Lise knew that if her mother couldn't bear this, she couldn't either. Even if this illness stopped, she'd never be normal. Normal people didn't have memories like hers. They didn't know pain like she did.

Monday, November 10, 2003, 7:13 PM

Julie had created a weapon.

She felt the world sway underfoot. All the success stories she had envisioned: effortlessly transporting food to starving children, sending supplies to astronauts without using fossil fuels, maybe even sending the astronauts themselves. Scientists with strong morals always harbored fears that their inventions could be used to hurt people, but she had been careful. There wasn't any military funding for this project, just herself, a shipping company, and some well-vetted private donors.

This was her child. Now it felt like her precious teenager had committed a massacre.

Marshall brought a chair over and guided Julie into it. The assistants were working at their own terminals. Someone was filling in another spreadsheet to track the objects; someone else was trying to crack the other ID codes. Julie wasn't clear who was doing what. It didn't matter. Nothing mattered.

"We should bring in some people to help," Marshall said quietly, crouching beside her. "We should call John."

With a violent shake of her head, Julie nearly shouted, "Don't call John." She started again. "Let's wait until tomorrow. I want to see if we can figure this out, and if we can't, we should shut it down as soon as possible. Then we can tell John about it."

She yanked herself up and retrieved a rolling whiteboard, stained and scarred by years of use. She'd work the problem. A suitably hydrated marker in hand, Julie drew boxes with arrows. Normally, she thought of multiverses as bubbles sprouting and dividing from themselves. That analogy didn't feel right. Electrical circuits crossed her mind. She drew, then erased and redrew and labeled. She stood back. A single plane, the simplest explanation.

"There's been nothing on the news?" she asked.

"Nothing appearing or disappearing, no."

"Unexpected meteor showers or anything?"

"No, nothing."

Julie nodded. She erased. One arrow was erroneous.

"You're thinking different time flows apply here?" Marshall asked quietly.

Julie nodded. "Items aren't transferring at a set interval. The requests must be issued as needed."

"Consciousness is at the destination, not at sending? How did you draw that conclusion?"

Julie didn't respond. She heard him walk over to the terminals.

"How could all this stuff be in any one place?"

"There's a story here," Allison replied. "You can see it. You see how the first batch of stuff is mostly food?"

"Baking ingredients," Spencer muttered.

"Then just before the ID switch, there are more weapons, convenience store items, and some random stuff."

"You have a theory for that?"

Allison shook her head, still facing her monitor. "Sounds like the origin is a strip mall in a neighborhood that's gone downhill."

Xiulan added, "Or a restaurant that's now like a guns and convenience store."

Marshall nodded. "Things have obviously gone wrong for the requester."

"And the recipient. Jesus hell, there's a machete in here."

He walked back to Julie and the whiteboard. "You have no machine drawn at either end of the destination or departure point."

"There's obviously something receiving and sending. A machine in the classic sense would be odd. Why would you send these specific items? Why would you build an entire machine to request them? A or C, or both, must have something I don't understand. D is where the real machine is. I think Gordon—or really, the master computer running this—is exploiting some sort of overlap or, I don't know, fluidity between these two universes and ours."

"Fluidity?"

Julie shrugged. "Coherence doesn't seem the right word. Maybe Gordon doesn't work here *because* there is no need for balancing here. Perhaps this system is only functioning because of entropy —Universes A and C have another system running in the opposite direction. It could be machines created in different galaxies in Universe A and C. Or it could be a naturally occurring wormhole that has matter passing through it—whoever is on the ends of this might not even know about this original exchange, or their universes are falling apart in some slowly horrible way and they don't have time to notice. Personally, I'm leaning toward a Kerr black hole, since these objects appear to be on a one-way trip. The two universes that needed to balance the matter exchange, we have nothing to exchange, so we're just exploited for Gordon in order to do so. Who knows."

"Sounds like a lot of what-ifs and maybes.

What changed with this experiment? What made it start working like this now?"

Julie returned to writing and shrugged. "On our end, we reduced potential interference, gave Gordon a new power supply, some fresh cables, rewrote some minor pieces of code. I have no idea why this happened now. I don't think it is anything we did. Something must have happened elsewhere."

"So, we can't control it," Marshall concluded.

Julie pointed to the box labeled Universe B. "I think Gordon is a relay between requests. Somewhere someone in D has invented the real teleportation machine. My guess is that requests are sent from Universe A, through us here at B, back to the master signal at Universe D. The master signal relies on us to maintain the transmission between Universe C and Universe A. We're a key link in this chain. I bet we can change the commands because they are passing through us. I'd like to start with the item ID numbers."

"Ok," Allison announced. "I know this isn't my field of expertise, but isn't it more probable that the machine is exploiting entanglement, reading the atomic structure of these objects and then recreating them at the destination, like we were trying to do? Is there really actual movement of matter going on here? Isn't that way, way, way more complicated and unlikely?"

"Yeah. This feels clumsy and complicated. But, imagine if trillions of atoms were suddenly reappropriated for a shotgun, then a handgun, then a knife. What would that kind of atomic movement cause to the surrounding environment? I'd imagine we wouldn't see any more requests, to say the least. I also think it is working, it is arriving at its destination, for the same reason. They're getting what they want, when they want it, enough to keep making the requests."

Marshall moved closer to the whiteboard, deep in thought. He turned to Julie and, keeping his voice low, asked, "Why aren't we Universe A?"

Allison chuckled. "A has all the power. They make requests, they get their demands. There can be only one."

"*Highlander*. Nice." Xiulan nodded as she typed.

Julie asked, "Someone print out the items we've got so far?"

The printer started warming up. Julie stared at the board.

"I still don't get Universe A. What is going on there? You can make a machine that teleports from another universe. It must be amazing. Yet you request baking goods? And handguns?"

Marshall didn't respond, staring at the whiteboard in thought. Julie detected skepticism from him, but she didn't mind. She didn't have a theory. She had data on a screen and her intuition, nothing more, to prove that anything was happening. The printer stopped. She walked across the room and retrieved the warm pages and a beige scotch-tape dispenser.

The first pages to go up were lists of baking ingredients, knives, and some other odds and ends. The shift to mostly weapons she marked with a highlighter, then stuck that page to the board. As it sat on the whiteboard, an entry jumped out at her.

"Huh . . . ," Julie said, leaning forward. Marshall leaned in likewise.

"What do you see?"

"It's nothing, just . . ." Julie looked back through the first pages. With a different highlighter, she started marking the margin beside certain entries.

"Vaseline? A thermometer. Baby wipes. Cough syrup. Paper towels. Pacifier. A kids' book?"

"My favorite book from when I was a kid, actually. Weird. And baby gear?"

"Yeah," Marshall replied hesitantly.

"There's some weapons before and in the middle of this stuff, but there's nothing like the baby stuff later."

"Does that mean something to you?"

"We were talking about these universes having different time coordinates earlier. What if this is all happening over decades? Here we have a relatively peaceful period, there's a kid or two to care for, and then here, it all goes to hell in a handbasket." Julie fell silent, seeing past the list in her hand, imagining the lives at the other end. The exchange of food and baby items between places, owned by one and needed by the other. So much like how she had intended the technology to be used—to help good people limited by their access to good things. Yet the innocence of the list fell to violence.

"Maybe we should bring John in on this," he said quietly.

She rolled her eyes. "No. Stop asking. John god-damn Fields can't be anywhere near this."

"Why not?" Marshall asked. "I thought you liked John."

"That was before I knew him better. Look, just let me get some work done. Give me a couple of hours."

Marshall stuffed his hands in his pockets and left slowly, looking around the lab with a thought-ful, concerned expression.

12

APRIL 9, 2013

6:31 PM

DANIEL WAS ALONE CLEANING THE SHOP. HE HAD started some dance music on his laptop, but the shuffle feature had picked a white-noise track he used to fall sleep sometimes. Too tired to go change it, he kept sweeping, lost in thought.

Uncle Joe had stopped speaking to him for weeks after their argument. Daniel tried apologizing a few more times, but his uncle would only hold up a hand in response. They'd pass each other silently, eat separately, and keep their eyes away from one another. Uncle Joe left for meetings a few times, leaving stressed but returning almost relaxed. In the last week or so, it had seemed things were better. Without knowing any details, Daniel guessed the men had forgiven his uncle.

The pressure lifted, they had started to pick up their routine again. Together they would clean the shop, stock the shelves and chuckle as best they could over the ghost's thefts. Though relieved to be on better terms with his uncle, Daniel held on to his concerns. He had always thought of his uncle as a good man who worked for bad people. Was he still good?

Moreover, Daniel had put his fingerprints all over the watch and given it back to the victim's family. If they went to the police, it wouldn't be difficult for a connected criminal, particularly one who owned cops, to figure out who gave the watch back.

Daniel looked back on his little research project with deep shame. His compassion, his attachment to the notion of sentimental belongings, had put his uncle in danger. The glee he had felt hopping down the steps of that suburban home had turned sour. It was just a watch, but he'd turned it into a weapon aimed at the only person he loved.

He finished sweeping and although it wasn't necessary, he dragged over the wheeled mop bucket. It took several trips from the sink in the back room to fill the bucket. It would've been easier to roll the bucket back, but he wasn't in the mood for efficiency. He had just started to mop when his uncle returned from the bar, red-faced and happy. Drunkenness seemed to be the only state that made him happy.

"Danny! Looks great in here!"

"Thanks, Uncle Joe. How was your date?"

Uncle Joe shrugged dramatically. "Nope. Oh well. But there was a pool tournament going on at the Three Kings, so I went over that way and won some money. Any moron could see the new guy was a pool shark. Tonight, I was that moron. I let him tease me a bit, and just when he was gonna switch it on, I said, so long!"

"Nice work, Uncle Joe," Daniel said with a smile, pushing the mop across the floor.

Joe dragged a metal folding chair to the middle of the floor and after a few unsuccessful attempts managed to unfold it. He plopped down and the metal creaked in protest. "Daniel. Did I ever tell you about the time the ghost stopped?"

"Stopped?" Daniel asked, wringing out the mop and rolling the bucket to a new spot on the floor.

"Yeah, lasted a year or two," his uncle began, but held up a hand while he belched. "'Scuse me. Then I lost a gun, or a sword, or something, and then another six months went by. Nothing! Then, it'd take some weird shit, too. Like a brush I had to clean the graffiti off the back door. Right out of my bucket, while I was using it! Me, standing out there like a jackass with a bucket of soapy water. Pissed me off. But then it'd stop again. No reason, plenty of stuff worth taking. Made me sad. It was a nice distraction, thinking about the ghost and all the shit it stole. This job sucks. Eh, you know how it is. Sad saps coming in, selling stuff, haggling over the prices of things like their lives depend on it. But the ghost is sort of apart from all this depressing shit. It was nice to wonder what the hell they needed all them sanitary napkins for, you know?"

Daniel laughed. "I think we know about that."

"Sure. Seemed like a lot, though. I'm just saying."

"It'd be fun to make a list of all the stuff the ghost takes."

"Yeah. Weird stuff. In the early days, it was crayons and kids' toys and diapers. Once they took toilet paper." Uncle Joe laughed. "Hey, I can see that, poor bastard."

Daniel had a question he wanted to ask, but he wasn't sure if his uncle being drunk made it more or less likely to get answered. The conversation was still pleasant. He decided it was worth the risk.

"Do the guys know about the ghost?"

Uncle Joe mulled the question over and finally nodded. "One of the bosses was here once, heard the pop, saw something go missing. He swore he saw the ghost that time. I've been here over twenty years, I never seen nobody, but this guy's here ten minutes and sees something. He swore it was a lady in a big white dress, hoop skirt and all that. I didn't see nothing. He told everybody that story. They don't like to come in here. Always make me come to them."

The last line was delivered with resentment, but Daniel knew better than to respond. He nodded as he pushed the bucket to the back room. "Do you think the ghost is, like, a girl or a guy?"

"Sanitary napkins?" His uncle laughed. "Come on, kid. Might be a really desperate guy with a lady friend, I suppose."

The two were silent for a moment. "Plus all the baby stuff in the early days." Uncle Joe's smile faded to a thoughtful frown. "Books, toys. But then all the weapons and first aid kits. And the baby stuff stopped. Used to go out to buy some diapers, leave them out on the shelves in case they needed it. Stupid, you know. But now, now I keep thinking it's someone in trouble, or someone scared. This country has gone to hell, but even we don't need all these guns and bullets all the time. Jesus. I hope it isn't a lady."

They sank into silence, Daniel cleaning as his uncle slumped sadly in the artificial light. "Do you want some water, Uncle Joe?"

"Nah, nah, you keep at it. I'll grab some milk upstairs. You finish up here, will you? Shut the lights off when you're done."

Uncle Joe rose unsteadily, returned the chair to its spot against the wall, and walked upstairs. Daniel heard him fumbling with the lock at the top before he entered their apartment.

Daniel folded up the chair and rolled the bucket to the back of the office. He flipped the cover on the peephole in the steel alley door and checked for lurkers. He hauled the door open, shoved a brick against it and dumped the murky water into the gravel. Alone in the darkness, he looked up at the sky. Helicopters were scrutinizing the landscape with their spotlights, flying slowly, sometimes circling. Sirens wailed in the distance. There were no stars.

He thought about what his uncle had said about the guns and about the ghost being someone in trouble. Joe didn't seem to realize they lived in the sort of place where a woman would be scared and might need weapons. Bricks and concrete and urine and garbage set the scene, and frightening people populated most of it. Daniel had lived in the suburbs before the pandemic. Back then the only garbage in the gutters were ice cream wrappers left by school kids walking home. From his backyard he could see the stars. When he and his dad went camping, they could see galaxies and planets. Here it was just a filmy haze from the light pollution. One day he would move back to the suburbs. Or maybe even the country. He wanted to see the stars again.

13

DECEMBER 23, 2020

5:18 PM

Lise walked down a residential street a few blocks from the beach. Older couples passed by, their white lapdogs jingling as they trotted along. She stepped into the street to let them by. The houses were small mansions wedged into parcels designed for compact beach houses. The setting was gloomy and romantic—rocky cliffs constantly battered by the sea, hills in the distance dotted with trees fanned away from the water by winds. A man in his sixties wearing bright yellow short-shorts ran by, glaring at her. Lise ignored him. Her destination was nearby.

Lise approached the walkway as a woman in a neighboring home peered out from the darkness. Lise ignored the examination and approached the smallest house on the block. It was meticulously maintained but spartan. Some of the other houses had lawn ornaments, exotic gardens, rarely used sports cars beneath car covers. But this house seemed folded within itself, as though it wished everyone else would go away.

She rang the doorbell. An odd hissing sound clicked off inside. Shuffling footsteps followed by muttering grew louder as the person approached the front door. Though it was still light enough outside, the interior and exterior lights came on. The door opened, the sound of the rubber sealant on the tile swooshing as it passed over the textured surface.

The older man standing before her was clearly too young for this place, though he looked considerably more aged than Lise had expected. She had prepared a speech, explaining who she was, what she wanted, and asking to talk for just a minute. Before she could speak, the man's eyes started watering.

"Julie? Is that you?" He stepped closer and his face blanched with fear. "Oh, no. Little Lise! Oh my God."

He moved his arms as if to give her a hug, but then paused, as if unsure whether she was real. Lise smiled and offered a hug.

He smelled like aftershave and laundry soap. That smell was familiar to Lise, a link to memories of her mother. Her tears dampened his cardigan. He laughed, wiped away his own tears and ruffled her dyed hair. "You can't fool me with this. You still look just like your mom."

"It's really good to see you, Dr. Fields."

. . .

An hour later, Lise and Dr. Fields were in an old lab. He had a lifetime lease on the building, he explained, and had refused to rent it to anyone else. It had been part of the physics department of the university, but with growing endowments, the school had replaced its labs and rendered this building obsolete. A research facility, even a dilapidated one, was terrifying to Lise, but his house wasn't safe. She let him lead the way.

Dr. Fields had been her mother's advisor in college, before she had abandoned her degree. Though he worked in the same field as her father, he had been closest with her mother. Lise felt safe with him. Yet when she prepared to speak, her prepared speech seemed immature. To compose herself , she focused on the abandoned lab. The fluorescent light in the ceiling was a final resting place for bugs and gathered dust. A few stray notebooks lay on random shelves; computers sat idle and obsolete under plastic covers on workstations. Trash cans still held bits of garbage.

"I wanted to know if my brother and sister have this disease and how they are doing. I don't care about Dad. And I know what happened to Mom . . . Of course I want to know why she and I have this . . . thing. But I need to know if Sophie and Elliot have it, if they caught it from me, somehow."

Dr. Fields shook his head. "No. No, they don't. Of course they don't."

"Thank God."

He didn't respond immediately. After rubbing his chin, he shook his head. "You know, after I finished my doctorate, I got to work with Amidore Huntington, who you haven't heard of. He was brilliant, and he had picked me to help him. I didn't have connections, but he picked me. It was a big honor. I helped him build vaccines. At least, I thought they were vaccines. He needed a mathematician to calculate certain things, and I suppose he knew a physicist wouldn't have the faintest clue about microbiology. I worked for him for a year before I found out my equations had been used to kill people. I thought of how proud my mother had been when I got that job. Her sickly boy, not only a college graduate, not only a scientist, but working with an eminent scientist, helping to save the world. We lost my brother to cancer, you know. It destroyed her. When I chose physics, she made me promise to never be one of those Oppenheimer types. My mother may have never had a formal education, but she was a sharp woman. Maybe she knew I'd fall into that trap no matter what she said. She knew I was too ambitious for my own good.

"Anyway, your mother and father were dating in college. I knew them both, and I was familiar with your father's reputation. I thought it was stupid, but I never said anything. I figured your mother wouldn't put up with him. But then, a couple years after graduating, she told me they were getting married. She was pregnant with you, of course, but I didn't know that then. I just knew she hadn't finished her studies like she had said she would. I knew I should intervene. But I had done this terrible thing. I had taken this job without scrutiny. So when your mother told me she was marrying your father, I felt like I couldn't say much, not about anything, really. To me, my reputation was gone."

Lise shook her head. "Mom respected you so much."

"Yes, well. She did marry your father, so perhaps her judgment wasn't particularly sound."

Lise wiped her eyes but tried to continue smiling. Fields reached over and gave her hand a squeeze. "You're so much like her. It's almost like your father wasn't involved at all. I know you shouldn't speak ill of the dead, but I can't say anything good about him. He wasn't half the scientist your mother was. He was out for himself, all the time, but he wasn't good enough to accomplish anything on his own." Fields's sad blue eyes, constantly moist with age, watered now. He blew his oversized nose into an embroidered handkerchief.

"Who . . . do you think killed him?"

"The Chinese were paying him. So were some other governments. He had his fingers in so many pies, you will never find out. I certainly don't know."

"I remember coming here with Mom to visit you."

Fields nodded and looked around. "That was

when your father was in charge of researching your mom's gift. You all came over here. It was fun, seeing what your mom could do."

"Not all fun, I think."

"No. Not all fun."

"That's all you guys did here? Research on the illness?"

"You call it an illness? Well, I suppose that's one way to look at it. Yes, we ran tests on her. Your mom helped design some of them. In fact, this was a fun thing we never figured out." Fields rose from his chair and retrieved a black box from a table.

"What is that?"

He let out a barking laugh. "This? This is a portable radio!"

Fields plugged it in and shook his head, still chuckling to himself. The radio let out a hiss of static.

"That's . . . neat," Lise said. The scientist laughed again.

"Normally, these things receive and translate radio waves into music, or talk shows, or whatever. But they didn't work around your mom, and they don't work around you. You've probably never heard a radio. They were out of date by the time you were born. Anyway, once you leave, this will start playing music."

Lise looked at the box in confusion. "Does that tell you anything about my illness?"

Dr. Fields returned to his seat. "Well, we studied the signal and found it was a data transmission. This is long before your time, but the internet used to require telephone lines. I always thought this sounded a bit like a dial-up modem. We analyzed the signal and found there was data encoded in it, but we couldn't crack it. With all the advances in computers now, I bet we could figure it out."

"It'd be nice to know what was in that data."

Dr. Fields raised a scruffy eyebrow at her very briefly. He resumed his look of concern and smiled. "If you wanted to, we could take a look. Only if you want to."

"You never found anyone else, then."

"Nope. Just you and your mom."

"So you never figured out . . . how . . . ?"

"How what, pumpkin."

Lise laughed, but the endearing term felt out of place.

"Oh, no. I think the radio is a clue. Your mother thought it was a wormhole, somehow. But without more research, we'll just never know."

Lise rose, plastering a smile on her face. "Can I help you home?"

"No, my dear, I drove us here, I can drive myself home, thank you. Before you go, though. Let me just say this one thing. Your father is gone. If you want to get to the bottom of this, the best place is right here. I'd be in charge. Nothing barbaric would go on. I'd keep you safe."

"I don't know."

"You could see Sophie and Elliot again. You

could live with them, and come here, figure out this out."

Lise gave him a kiss on his soft, sunken cheek.

He smiled grimly, but nodded. "Take this, honey. I promised your mom I'd watch you, but I guess I can only give you money." He pressed an envelope heavy with cash into her hand. "Go on now, child. Go someplace safe. We'll see each other soon."

14

NOVEMBER 10, 2003

8:40 PM

"You can't change the IDs?" Julie asked.

"Nope," Allison affirmed. "Just ignores the command. I can add items to existing requests, but I can't remove items from requests."

"Transfers, you mean?" Xiulan asked.

"Well, shit, I suppose. No reason to get all pedantic here when we don't know for sure what is going on," Allison replied testily.

Xiulan, oblivious to the tone, leaned back in her chair. "What if guns aren't guns there."

"What?"

"The elements might be different. Gunpowder might not exist. A gun there might not be a gun."

"You think someone is ordering hundreds of, what, supersoakers?" Allison replied.

"There are the knives, too," Spencer added with softness.

"Yeah," Xiulan muttered sadly.

Julie only half-listened. She was thinking of other modifications they could attempt when a distinctive knock on the door froze her thoughts. Julie looked up sharply, as did the researchers all bent over their computers.

Dr. John Fields sauntered into the lab, his outfit expensive, authoritative yet casual. He glanced at the working scientists. Marshall followed behind, looking ashamed and bewildered.

"Heard old Gordo's been making some mischief!" John announced, striding over the yellow barrier tape, taking up the apple from the pad and biting into it.

"We're getting some odd data output, nothing conclusive," Julie said, removing the printouts from the whiteboard. Xiulan noticed and minimized her spreadsheet, and kicked Allison's ankle so she would do the same.

"I assume that Marshall got you up to speed?" Julie inquired, looking at Marshall with a fierce demand. He shook his head no.

Dr. Fields threw the apple away. "Just bits and pieces. Got wind of this through the other labs, said you guys were running something that was causing interference. That you had your researchers running around with radios, asking questions."

Julie shrugged. "We're not really sure what's going on. I wanted to wait until we had some perspective before bothering you."

Dr. Fields stepped away from Gordon, smiling at Julie in a way that made her uneasy. "It's a nice little coincidence. Some people from DARPA are in town. They asked if we were running anything here that might interest them."

"I'm not sure that we do," Julie said, her face hardening.

"Come on, Julie. Don't start being modest with me. I've known you too long for that! No one's gotten a teleportation machine to do anything but transfer quantum states! This one is transmitting data across the whole building!"

"It's causing interference."

At this, Dr. Fields glanced around at the computer monitors. Xiulan had a piece of software that simulated an FM radio taking up her entire screen. She was making notes in a spreadsheet, seeming to scrutinize the graph. Spencer, as usual, had a screen filled with code. He seemed to be writing, but Julie was pretty sure it was for show. Allison wasn't pretending to work at all. She had her chair spun around to face the three senior scientists. Chewing her gum and squeezing a stress ball, she eyed them with blank interest.

Dr. Fields allowed a scowl to momentarily cross his face. "It looks like you folks aren't too busy. I think I'll give those guys a ring, see if they are up for a late-night visit. Might be worth having some folks with more relevant experience look at this."

Marshall cleared his throat. "It'd be best if we wait 'til morning. Jumping in now is going to cause more chaos." In a lower voice, he added, "Plus, we need to think about team morale."

Fields let out a single loud laugh and slapped

the younger man's shoulder. "Morale. That's rich. Jules, get me a coffee, will you? I'll be in Marshall's office."

The two men left the lab, leaving Julie standing in the middle of the room, shivering with fury.

"Boss?" Spencer asked quietly.

Julie nodded, as if he had made an important point. Speaking softly, she said, "Encrypt our data. Move it somewhere off our server. Weren't we accidentally given permissions for some random storage drive?"

"Yes, the English department," Xiulan said. "I used it to check my grade last week."

"Great, move it all there when it's locked up. Name it something bland and technical that they'll never look at. Spence, can you change the modify date on the files?"

Spencer had turned back to his console but Julie saw him nod.

"Allison, go destroy all our hard copies. You'll have to avoid the hallway security cameras."

"Sure, I'll just go to the bathroom with the papers stuffed in my bra. I've done it before."

Julie prepared a question but thought better of it. "Great."

Turning away from the researchers, Julie faced her whiteboard. She picked up an eraser reluctantly. There wasn't anything there she couldn't replicate. Her eyes glanced over her formulas, diagrams, and other information. With a swipe, she started erasing, and continued until it was gone.

Allison, making crinkling sounds as she walked, grabbed the key to the bathroom and left the lab. Xiulan finished working on her computer, locked the screen, asked Spencer if he needed help. He ignored her, so she left, presumably to check on Allison.

The door hadn't fully closed behind her when Marshall rushed into the room, shutting the door quickly.

"It's too late. They're already here."

15

APRIL 10, 2013

4:18 AM

THE MUSIC COMING THROUGH DANIEL'S HEADPHONES was loud and fast. It wasn't something he particularly enjoyed, but it helped him focus when he was in a hurry. After mopping the floors, he had found vomit on the front door and stayed late to clean it off, and now he only had an hour to finish his Social Dynamics homework and run to the bus stop. He balanced his textbook on his lap and typed out the assignment, hoping his teacher would review it by email. He wouldn't have time to finish it before school. He wasn't excited at the idea of taking the computer on the bus, but that was a problem for later. Right now he had to churn out answers.

IN TALCOTT PARSONS' THEORY OF FUNCTIONALISM, WHAT FORM OF RELATIONSHIP EXISTS BETWEEN A PERSON AND THEIR POSSESSIONS?

. . .

Daniel stared blankly at the question, then looked through his book for the section on Parsons. As he skimmed, he heard a sound that didn't match the pattern of his song. He lowered one headphone from his ear. The knock at the door was loud, strong, and insistent. His uncle was still asleep upstairs.

"Open up, Joe," the muffled voice on the other side of the door said with no small degree of menace. "It's Reggio."

Daniel knew the name Reggio. It belonged to one of the men Uncle Joe worked with. He did not want to go to the door. He thought about waking his uncle, but didn't want him to get hurt. He grabbed the keys to the office door and thought about getting the baseball bat from under the counter. Instead, he grabbed the mace and turned on his phone to record audio, and put both in his pockets. He locked the office door behind him and hid the keys on a shelf. The knock came again, louder this time.

Daniel's knees were shaking as he walked to the door. While passing a group of shelves near the wall, he noticed random empty places. It looked like a quarter of the stock was gone. He paused, confused. He didn't hear anything or see movement from the shelves, so he continued to the door.

Before he reached the lock, he heard the sound of keys. The door flung open onto a giant wall of a man who almost blocked the two goons accompanying him.

Daniel stared at the man's bloodshot eyes, dark tattoos, and foul teeth.

"Where's Joe," Reggio growled.

"I, uh . . ." Daniel couldn't seem to form words, but managed to shake his head in confusion.

"That's fine. We're here for you anyway."

With a single, effortless movement, Reggio pushed. Daniel's body flew backwards through the air and crumpled on the floor. He noticed the pleasant fragrance of wood soap, fresh from his work. One of the thugs behind Reggio stepped forward, smiling gleefully.

16

DECEMBER 24, 2020

2:54 AM

STARTLED, LISE WOKE TO A CREAK OUTSIDE HER motel room. She rolled out of bed away from the window. To her sleep-deadened ears, she had been totally silent. Without moving, she listened carefully.

She had picked this motel because it wasn't busy, and chose her room by checking the four sets of stairs. The ones to the right of her window were the noisiest. The guy working the counter didn't seem to care that she had a preference. It made her wonder if people often demanded specific rooms. Lise had thought about leaving broken glass outside the door, like she had seen in movies, but decided that was going too far.

She hadn't undressed for bed and was still wearing shoes as she squatted on the industrial carpet, hiding from the door and window, listening. Two men's voices, very soft, passed through the single-pane glass window before her. A shadow blocked out part of the light coming under the door. Lise wasn't frightened. She'd put a chair under the door handle and four adhesive baby locks from the hardware store on the window. They could break the glass, but it'd take time. She had a way out.

She moved quietly into the bathroom and shut the door, securing more baby locks along with the regular lock. Lise took a breath. She had painstakingly tied knots in a length of rope earlier in the day. She looped the rope around the base of the toilet and the shower frame, then tied it. She had meant to do this before going to bed, but there wasn't time to beat herself up over it now. She put on her gloves and waited.

The envelope from Dr. Fields sat on the countertop. She almost put it in her bag, but paused, recalling the sense of force in his affection and concern. "We'll see each other soon." *Why had he said that?*

She thought of him weeping over her mother, his frailty, his outstretched arms when he first saw her.

She opened the envelope slowly. Stacks of cash were tightly grouped together, but there was something else: a small rectangle in the middle of the stack. A tracking device. Lise tore it out then flipped through the cash. It might be fake, or the serial numbers might be registered. She cursed under her breath and threw the bills into the sink.

She put her ear to the bathroom door. The men were still speaking quietly, accompanied by a new sound—the faint hiss of static. It was time to go.

17

NOVEMBER 10, 2003

8:47 PM

Julie looked at Marshall in horror and confusion. Spencer only replied, "Buy me some time."

"How are they . . . He said he was going to call them?"

Marshall looked out the small window in the door and shook his head. "I don't know, but can we disable Gordon somehow? How do we disconnect it?"

"We can shut it down, but they can just turn it back on," Julie muttered. "All the plans for Gordon were submitted, there are too many copies. They can just rebuild it."

"We need to make it stop working, but make it look like it's still working. Can we change any of the location codes? Like, maybe make the supply source a desert or field or something?"

Julie shook her head. "Those seemed to be locked in."

The sounds of expensive shoes and men's

laughter echoed through the empty hallway, growing louder as they approached. Marshall discreetly looked back out the window. "Not much time."

"Shit," Julie muttered, furiously thinking, but the switch from analyzing Gordon to breaking him was impossible.

"Done," Spencer announced. He turned on his screensaver, pushed away from his desk, grabbed a stale cupcake, and put his feet up on a table in the middle of the room. Without further explanation, he began to eat in a pose of utter laziness. Marshall squinted at him. Julie frowned. The door opened.

Dr. Fields announced with a forced smile, "Fellas, you know Marshall. This is Dr. Julie Coyne. This little lady is a protégé of mine. And over here is the man of the hour, Gordon."

The men nodded at Julie, exchanged a bemused glance with one another, then followed Fields to the machine. Spencer glanced casually at them, then turned back to Marshall.

"So, the defender can't pass back to his keeper in normal regulation play. But they were allowing pass-backs as long as the player didn't use his or her foot. Like, a knee was okay. Or a header. It made no sense."

"That doesn't make sense," Julie said without having to feign confusion.

Marshall said, "Sure. It's a smaller field, right? Maybe it's just an accommodation for that."

Spencer shook his head and held up one finger.

"They were still going by standard off-sides rules, using the halfway line. It's not like they were changing all the important stuff for a smaller field. I heard some league was using the box as the boundary, but that's just ridiculous."

Julie allowed their conversation to conceal her observation of the DARPA men. They looked skeptical— Fields was pushing too hard, giving off the air of a used-car salesman. *He always tries too hard,* she thought.

"Wait, you can rotate keepers? Is there a limit? Does it count as a sub?"

Spencer grabbed another cupcake, unwrapping it in between expressive gestures. "Nope. Just swap them out whenever, as many times as you want."

Marshall shook his head gravely. "Why even bother playing at that point."

"What formation are they playing? Four-four-two, or something different?" Julie asked.

The two men paused and looked at her with admiration.

Allison opened the door and looked with some perplexity at the scene before her. She started to move toward her computer, but Julie motioned her to the table with her eyes.

"Shit, Spence, did you eat all the cupcakes again?" Allison muttered.

"Jules," Dr. Fields called, "Come over here and explain the changes you made to Gordon that helped him work."

"Helped him work? What do you mean?"

The DARPA men looked annoyed. Fields glared. The conversation amongst her co-researchers fizzled out.

"The transmissions. Show them," he hissed.

"Oh, that. That stopped." Julie shrugged, picking up someone's coffee and taking a sip. She could see the liquid shiver as her hand shook slightly.

"If it's all right with you, we'd like to see your software," one of the DARPA men said, his tone cold. "John was saying that there were some interesting data points."

Julie shrugged. "Spence, can you show the gentlemen what we have?"

Spencer nodded, brushed the crumbs off his hands, and pushed his rolling chair back to his terminal. Marshall and Allison, along with the three DARPA men, followed. Fields moved beside Julie, the two alone behind the group.

Julie saw his plastered smile and felt his fury as he approached. She stood casually, hoping Spencer had a plan. Dr. Fields grabbed her arm, squeezing her until his knuckles turned white. He snarled through clenched teeth, "Stop screwing around, Jules. I'll end you if you embarrass me. I'll fucking end you."

Julie gasped in pain and shock. The initial surprise quickly turned to rage.

"Screw you, John," she whispered, digging her foot into the flesh at the top of his dress shoe. She felt a satisfying crackle and hoped she had broken something. The older man released her.

Julie moved away, trying to pretend nothing had happened. She hadn't composed herself yet when one of the DARPA men turned and shook his head. "It's weird. I guess we could take a closer look, but I'm pretty sure there is nothing going on here."

18

APRIL 10, 2013

4:24 AM

"Knife or gun? Which one?"

"Boss doesn't want the place messy. No knife. Carlo, grab the tarp."

Carlo, a much smaller man with a bear tattoo on his neck, had a blank face as he emerged from Reggio's shadow. Daniel was almost able to get up now, the tide of dizziness ebbing. Before he could rise, the weapon man pushed him back to the ground.

"Not yet, sweet cheeks. Gotta get your bed all ready before we tuck you in."

Daniel finally understood. He pushed his hand into his pocket, searching frantically for the can of mace, but found only the hole he hadn't mended yet.

"Shit," he said aloud.

"Yeah, you messed up, kid." Reggio nodded. "Givin' away stuff that didn't belong to you. It's your uncle's fault, really. He shoulda told you we was just dumping stuff for it to disappear. Oh well!"

The large tarp was laid flat. The second man and the man called Carlo lifted Daniel onto the noisy, shiny blue material.

"Nothing should get on the stuff. Make sure the splatter hits the empty wall. I got some paint in the trunk."

Panic and terror dominated Daniel's thoughts, yet this sentence struck him as peculiar. *There aren't empty walls in here…*

The second man opened his eyes wide. He reached back to retrieve his gun from a concealed holster. He looked down at his empty hand, then glared at Carlo. Carlo shrugged, shook his head, then took out his own gun. The second man snatched it from him and turned the muzzle on Daniel.

Daniel had been held up before. In movies, people wrestled the gun away or ran away or dodged. He wasn't that daring. He always stayed still, stared at the perfect circle of the barrel, two shades of darkness with a glint of silver, and complied with demands. Usually, handing over his wallet, cell phone, shoes, and backpack made the barrel go away. These guys were just going to kill him, so he did nothing. He just stared, wondering if he'd see a little bit of fire in the dark tube when they shot him.

. . .

Daniel never found out. The gun disappeared.

19

DECEMBER 24, 2020

3:04 AM

LISE PICKED UP THE HEAVY COILS OF ROPE AND opened the bathroom window. She saw no movement. She tossed the coils to the ground, then paused. Still no movement. She threw her backpack down into a bush against the building. As quietly as she could, she climbed onto the toilet and stuck her leg out the window. Straddling the sill, she paused again. The door to the motel room started to thud. They'd picked the lock and realized the door was reinforced. It was only a matter of time before they walked around the building.

The feeling of pure fear reemerged. Lise swallowed it down, trying to use the extra motivation as she began her descent. The toilet and shower frame groaned under her weight. Keeping her sneakers on the wall, she climbed down with quick determination. Though she was wearing gloves, the sharp, uneven stucco against her knuckles was agony. She had to keep going. She had to hold on tight.

A sound of electronic hissing grew louder from below. She glanced down. The men waiting for her seemed both afraid of her falling and angry at her for trying to escape. She felt the vibration of one of them grabbing the rope.

"Get down here, missy."

She closed her eyes, trying not to cry, her muscles burning as she clung to the rope. The cutting, the threats, the horrific videos, the sleep deprivation, the bright lights of the lab were coming for her.

One of the men below her shouted in alarm. "Watch out!"

20

THE CONFUSION ON ONE THUG'S FACE WAS MIRRORED on the faces of the other two. In the office on Daniel's right, a plank of wood held up by two stacks of books clattered to the ground. The books were gone. Daniel craned his neck to see the rest of the store. An entire shelf disappeared; the usual solitary *pop* was now firecrackers in a garbage bin. The men rocked back on their heels, terrified.

Items suddenly vanished all around them, not just from the shelves or the walls, but from the men, too—their sunglasses, shoes, belts, jewelry. The pawn shop was quickly being depleted.

The men ran from the shop in terror. Daniel sat for a moment, fascinated by the items blinking out of existence all around him. His uncle was shouting upstairs and he realized it must be happening up there as well. He got up, locked the front door, and put the heavy security bar in place.

Shelves were emptying to the sounds of popping all around him. Through the security window in the office, he could see his uncle staring in disbelief.

"It sounds like hail."

21

DECEMBER 24, 2020
3:07 AM

LISE OPENED HER EYES AND SAW THINGS FALLING from the sky around her. Books, toys, canned food. There was the familiar snapping sound and the lingering smell, but more intense.

Bracing herself, she looked down. The men were being pelted by the objects and had backed away. One was bleeding from a cut on his head. Guns were falling, too. The hail was variable. It seemed as though five items at a time appeared in a circle around her, then after a second or two, five more would appear. For the first time, she thanked her disease.

She climbed down quickly, almost effortlessly, eager to reach the weapons that had always been so repugnant to her. She was going to get away. The ground met her feet and she grabbed her backpack from the top of a bush. Items continued to appear in an invisible circle beyond her outstretched arms, all around her. They blinked into existence, suspended in midair by their own improbability, before they were caught by gravity's momentum and struck the floor. The grass was littered with broken pottery, paper towels, books, and shattered glass. The men who had been waiting for her stayed back in shock.

Lise ignored them and scanned the ground. A can of pepper spray shone in the spotlight's glare, and a handgun. She picked it up reluctantly; the guns were not always loaded.

Mace and gun in hand, Lise ran along the side of the building toward the train tracks across the street. A man jumped out at her and she shrieked. He reached out to grab her, but fell back with a cry, his arm struck by a heavy metal doorstop in the shape of an animal.

She continued to run as items appeared with cascading pops. Soap, a cell phone, a textbook, a carton of milk, and a pair of men's shoes materialized and clattered to the ground. A few seconds later, a box of pens, a doll, a cartoon-character alarm clock, a knife, and a book of matches appeared. Lise regretted that she was leaving a trail, not that it mattered. The men were easily keeping up with her. The objects were keeping them at a distance, but it was going to be impossible to hide.

The crisscross pattern of the six-foot metal fence lining the train tracks was finally clear. Black sedans appeared around the corner on the otherwise deserted street. She checked both ways before rushing across to the tracks. It was only when she had navigated the trench that she saw old, drooping razor wire at the top. Lise jogged alongside, looking at the coils, searching for a wide enough gap. At a spot where one coil was shorter than the next, she climbed the fence, feeling it wobble under her weight, ignoring the men who were calling to her.

It was going to be painful. Lise removed her backpack and tried to rest it on top of the wire. The men were below her on the ground now, shouting incoherently. Lise grazed her leg as she tried to arch it high over a coil, aiming for the gap unsteadily. She bit back the pain and paused, astride the fence, sitting on her backpack.

"Come on, you got it," she said to herself.

Taking a deep breath, she lifted her other leg to bring it to the inside of the fence. The movement made the fence shake, freeing her backpack and causing her to slide into the open air. Lise watched her leg pass through the gap in the coil unharmed. She had just enough time to congratulate herself before she hit the ground.

The wind was knocked out of her. She gasped, waiting for her lungs to fill. The buckle of her backpack hit her tooth and blood pooled in her mouth. The absurdity would have been amusing if not for the men chasing after her. Still dizzy and out of breath, she took out the handgun and lazily pointed it at her pursuers. She pulled the trigger. To her surprise, it fired. The men dropped to the ground and rolled into the trench.

Items were still appearing around her as she

rose to her feet and grabbed her backpack. She paused to see if anything else useful had fallen before she clambered to the edge of the train tracks. Up ahead, the darkness was swallowed by a commuter train tunnel passing through a grassy hill. At this time of night, the tunnel was quiet and ominous.

Shots ricocheted off the ground in the distance. Lise ducked her head and ran clumsily as several male voices shouted. She stole a glance back and saw that several men were wrestling the gunman to the ground as another climbed the fence after her.

She ran into the tunnel, darkness growing around her as objects bounced off the gravel and train tracks. She had tried to explore this place the day before, but an oncoming train had chased her away. In her brief survey, she had seen a yellow metal ladder bolted to the curved wall that reached up and out of the tunnel.

The man behind her made it over the fence, hit the ground, and began running loudly but quickly. Lise's legs and feet were starting to strain. The darkness was growing denser. She could make out the edges of the tunnel and the glint of the tracks, but no ladder. In her memory, the ladder was much closer to the entrance. *Where is it?* she thought in panic. More objects appeared, including a flashlight. She didn't bother to reach for it.

"Stop, dammit!" the man behind her shouted.

Lise thought of her mother. *If they catch me, I've got at least one bullet left.*

Her shoulder struck the ladder and she dropped her gun. Without looking back, she darted upwards, but not quickly enough. The man reached through the hailstorm and grabbed her leg. Lise kicked, frantic to escape—yet she was so tired. Her fingers threatened to give way. More things, indistinct in the darkness, bounced off of him. Lise hooked her arm around the ladder and reached into her pocket desperately.

Her fingers found the can and twisted the nozzle with her thumb. She sprayed in the general direction of her captured leg.

The man's grip gave way, his cry still echoing in the tunnel when Lise reached the top. She opened the hatch and collapsed. *Close it, damn you. Close it,* she told herself, but she lay paralyzed beside the opening. A dictionary covered in cream linen fell into her lap, its foil letters and decorations glinting in the pale light. She heard the thuds of heavy shoes on the ladder. Without aiming, Lise lobbed the giant book at him. A satisfying jumble of sounds announced his fall, followed by silence. Lise closed the hatch and staggered away.

22

NOVEMBER 11, 2003

9:04 PM

JULIE HIT **ENTER**.

The command to shut down Gordon was complete.

"So he's done now," Allison said with a sigh.

"He's done here and now," Xiulan pointed out.

"Right. It could be hours before the actual movement of stuff for the other universes stops."

"Or years," Marshall added.

"Or yesterday. Freaky," Xiulan said.

Julie removed her glasses and pushed away from the computer. She put her head in her hands, hot tears flowing into her palms as she tried not to sob out loud. Marshall's hand on her back barely registered.

The DARPA men and Dr. Fields were long gone. Fields had glared at her with murderous hatred before he slammed the door behind him. Julie expected to be fired soon. It didn't matter. This project was over.

Marshall knelt on the floor next to her chair,

trying to get her to look at him. The younger researchers wandered away to give them privacy.

"Hey. Julie. Come on, don't! You can do this again. Gordon 2.0."

"I don't know what we did."

"You almost invented teleportation, Julie," he said firmly. "That's amazing."

She looked at him with a smile. "Almost. Yeah, I guess almost is about my speed."

Encouraged, Marshall gave her shoulder a squeeze. "Let's go get some drinks and talk about Gordon 2.0."

They rose, and Julie wiped her face with her sleeve as she returned her blue glasses to her cubby, exchanged them for her black frames. "First, we get drunk. And I get fired. Then Gordon redux."

He laughed. "Yeah, obviously after we get fired. Come on, guys, Three Kings has a drink special tonight, and a pool tournament. Might be fun to watch. Just don't play anyone, bunch of sharks there."

Xiulan shook her head. "I'm too young."

"We'll do that sports bar around the corner, then. The one by the comic shop."

Everyone began their departure routine. Julie grabbed her stuff and walked over to Gordon. Nearby was the portable radio Xiulan and Allison had brought in. She turned it on and the sounds of a boy band came over the airwaves. She shut it off.

Xiulan, Spencer, and Allison left the room

laughing loudly, the women mercilessly teasing Spencer about his soccer knowledge. Marshall waited for Julie at the door, hands in his pockets.

Julie shut off the power strips, looking around at the room with finality. As Marshall opened the door for her, she looked at him in the soft glow of the hall light.

Without giving it any thought, she kissed him, taking in his taste and gentle fragrance of his skin. When they parted, she smiled at him and ran her hand over the stubble on his face. He looked pleased but startled.

Julie laughed and shook her head, walking away from him. She hadn't gone far before he caught up and took her hand in his, giving it a squeeze. They left the laboratory without letting go.

23

APRIL 10, 2013

6:03 AM

UNCLE JOE HAD SUGGESTED THEY PACK, BUT DANIEL insisted on just taking the money from the safe and the register. The ghost had his shoes and he didn't want to lose the rest of his clothes. Items were still winking out of existence when they reached the vacant alley.

"Be careful of broken glass," Joe said.

"This isn't the first time I've had my shoes stolen."

Daniel had meant it as a joke, but he could see his uncle looked downcast.

"I know this isn't what your mom and dad would've wanted for you. I'm sorry."

Daniel shrugged. "The world's gone to shit. I think they just wanted someone to look out for me the best they could. And you've been great, Uncle Joe."

They stopped speaking as Daniel avoided rusted nails and suspicious puddles. They reached a charity store and tugged on the door before noting the time.

"This is Andy's shop. He lives upstairs. Wait here." Uncle Joe walked around to the back and soon appeared inside the store with an old man holding an enormous key ring. They shopped alone but quickly, eager to replace their missing items and leave town. As they waited to pay, Daniel had an uncomfortable thought.

"Uncle Joe, do you still have your wedding ring?"

Joe's face went ashen as he dug around his neck in panic. His thick fingers found the necklace and he spun the chain violently until he found the ring. The saint medallion had disappeared.

"Thank God. Oh, thank God." Joe clutched the ring with tears in his eyes, laughing quietly. "Took her pendant, but not the ring or the necklace. It's just goddamn weird. What about stuff from your moms and pops?"

"No. The cops didn't let me take anything."

They hadn't discussed their next steps. They had to leave as soon as possible. Joe's bosses weren't going to give up just because their henchmen had been scared off. They'd expect Joe to pay one way or another.

Daniel and Joe took the bus to the train and bus transit center. They looked at the board of destinations.

"Anything jump out at you?" Joe asked.

Daniel smiled. "How about Colorado? Or Montana?"

Joe laughed heartily. "Live out in the wilderness, eh? Sure, why not."

"We'll be able to afford something with what we have."

"True."

They boarded the Grand Junction-Denver bus. Uncle Joe looked relieved, somehow, but Daniel felt some regret. If today had gone normally, he'd be getting feedback from his Social Dynamics professor. He'd have gone to the library to study for his midterm. Maybe in a couple of years, he would have graduated from a prestigious university. But that was all over now.

"You know what? It's going to be nice seeing some stars again," Joe said with a satisfied sigh.

Daniel smiled. *Stars*, he thought. *We're going to see some stars.*

24

DECEMBER 24, 2020

4:55 AM

LISE HAD STOPPED RUNNING AN HOUR AGO, allowing herself the privilege of walking quickly. She rested briefly on occasion, eager to get as far away as she could. She gathered useful things from what appeared around her, but now her backpack and pockets were full. Then, suddenly, things stopped appearing. A strange sensation came over her. Not loneliness, exactly. It was as though she had lost connection. Even without testing it, she knew she couldn't bring over anything right now. There was no relief in the sensation. It could start again, at any time.

Lise continued north. The wilderness of the San Bruno Mountain State Park would run out. Eventually she'd reach San Francisco, where Kee lived. Where Sophie and Elliot lived.

When she'd still believed Dr. Fields would help her, seeing her siblings had seemed an obvious next step. Now she walked alone in the forest toward Kee, her best path to escape. Escape to where? Fear had propelled her this far, but now that it was ebbing, she had trouble finding fresh motivation.

Her primary goal in life, to stay alive, no longer seemed enough. She knew now no one could replicate her illness, even those desperate to profit from it. They couldn't understand it. There was no cure.

It was this thought that finally paralyzed her. Exhausted and overcome, she collapsed to the ground. The perfect darkness of the forest embraced her. She sat on the mossy floor with a rock digging into her thigh. Wind whispered through the trees above. There was no point in going on. She was completely alone.

To deepen her misery, she thought of little Sophie, who had loved dinosaurs. She thought of the way her hair shone in the daylight, little flecks of red appearing in the sun. She remembered how she preferred saltine crackers to cookies, and the stern resolution with which she had approached potty training. She thought of Elliot's scar on his cheekbone from falling into the coffee table, how his light-up sneakers were too small but he insisted on wearing them anyway, and how much he loved the wind in his face, even when the wind was just a breath from someone who loved him. Lise was crying when she remembered his reaction when she invented his favorite book out of thin air. The story of a small train, struggling to be more, failing but ultimately persevering, had spoken to him.

Lise felt ashamed now, sitting on the cold earth.

Sophie and Elliot were alive. Even if she could not see them, even if they never knew her again, to live for them would be enough. What luck to have someone left to love.

The self-pity drained away. She rose from the forest floor and pulled the straps of her backpack tight. The sun would rise in a few hours. She had to keep moving.

25

JUNE 2, 2140

9:14 AM

"DAMN. CONNECTION LOST," CALLED A STATION manager in the dark control room.

The cylinder projected on the wall slowed rotation. Object names that had filled the list, displayed in the cylinder, had slowed until it finally stopped. An image of three bubbles filled with galaxies, each separate yet attached to one another, occupied the center. Above, a sphere of greater size and detail, broadcasted a harsh red line to the trio.

"Confirmed intermediary disconnect," a second voice called.

A man sitting at the control desk turned to the room. "We maintained the connection for five seconds?"

"Yep."

"Good. The connection between departure and destination still stable?"

"Yes. Looks like we had some noise and minor time synch flaws, probably from the output volume at the end. They're balanced now."

"Alright. We can come back to that sample if necessary, but let's table it for now. We used a lot of power to run this sequence; five seconds isn't nearly long enough. Resourcing, do we have anything similar? Another triplet we can plug in? I'd like to run another test before my next meeting."

"Found one," a young woman's voice called. "Looks almost identical. Same location and time coordinates."

"All right. Let's establish connection and see how long it holds."

ABOUT THE AUTHOR

Norah Woodsey is the author of *Lifeless, When the Wave Collapses,* and *The Control Problem.* After careers in the finance and tech industries, she has dedicated herself to creating fiction. Her subjects of intense interest but not quite expertise include history, physics, genetics, sociology and gender studies. The product of four generations of Brooklynites, she now resides on the wrong coast with her family.

norahwoodsey.com